Tales of Oescienne

Volume One

-Conquer the Castle-
-The Spirit Stone Ring-
-Fire and Ice-

By Jenna Elizabeth Johnson

TALES OF OESCIENNE
VOLUME ONE

———

CONQUER THE CASTLE
THE SPIRIT STONE RING
FIRE AND ICE

CONTENTS

Tales of Oescienne
Volume One

-Conquer the Castle-
-The Spirit Stone Ring-
-Fire and Ice-

-Conquer the Castle-

"Master Hroombra!" Jahrra yelled over her shoulder from inside the Castle Guard Ruin as she dug around in an old trunk. "Are these the only old clothes you have lying around?"

It was a stupid question, Jahrra knew that, but she cringed as she held up the old, age-yellowed shirt and leggings. *Where on Ethöes did he get these?* she wondered. They looked like something a noble would have worn a hundred years ago.

As Jahrra contemplated the antique clothing, her guardian walked through the dragon's entrance of their home, blocking out the light for a moment as he came to stand over her.

"Your teacher's note said old, white clothing," he said blandly when he saw what she was doing.

Jahrra dropped the clothes back into the trunk and scowled at the Korli dragon. "Yes, *old*," she emphasized, "not ancient!"

"Well, that is all I have."

Jahrra sighed heavily and started digging through the trunk again. She could use some of her own clothes, but she didn't want them to get stained in the game of Conquer the Castle she and her classmates would be participating in the next day. She would have to make do with what she found in the trunk. It held not just the two pieces she had found earlier, but an entire wardrobe of garments, nearly all of them well-tailored and of a high quality.

They ranged greatly in size, but none of them were so big that she couldn't fit into them. She also realized that they were boy's clothes since there wasn't a single dress among the lot. *Thank goodness,* she thought.

She leaned back on her knees and studied the pile from a short distance. Yes, where had her mentor acquired these clothes? At first glance she had assumed they were costumes. Of course, why the dragon Hroombramantu would have costumes was just as puzzling as why he might have a wardrobe more fitting for a Nesnan or Resai elf.

"Ah," Hroombra said over Jahrra's shoulder, startling her out of her contemplation, "a fine choice."

He nodded towards the long white shirt and leggings Jahrra had set aside before he'd come into the room.

"Master Hroombra," she started, ignoring his observation, "why do you have all these clothes anyway?"

The great dragon was standing behind her, but for a moment, only a moment, she thought she felt him tense up. She turned her head and furrowed her brow at him. He was very still and a dark look seemed to have occupied his face, but in the next breath he brightened up a bit and said, "They belonged to a past student of mine."

Jahrra's eyebrows arched at that.

Hroombra merely nodded. "Though the general presence of dragons is frowned upon in this day and age, there was a time when our wisdom was sought out by those wishing to educate their children. I like to currently think of myself as retired." He gave her an amused look. "But I once had several pupils."

Jahrra held up a rather gaudy short coat, sewn from dark green velvet and embellished with golden thread and beads.

Conquer the Castle

"And were some of your past pupils royalty?" she teased, flapping the coat about in a haughty way.

The slight twitch of Hroombra's mouth could have been rather telling, but before Jahrra could decipher whether it was an acknowledgement of her statement or a mere reaction to something he found humorous, a familiar voice called from outside.

"Jahrra! You up?"

Jahrra dropped the coat onto the unkempt pile and raced for the door.

"Yes!" she answered as she met her best friend, Scede, at the door. Gieaun, his sister and her other best friend, was just behind him.

"Did you find anything to wear for tomorrow?" he asked, crossing his arms and trying to peer over her shoulder.

"Ugh," Jahrra moaned as she rolled her eyes and grabbed his sleeve, pulling him outside to join Gieaun.

"For some strange reason, Master Hroombra has a trunk full of boy's clothes that belonged to an old student of his. I found something in there."

Gieaun beamed. "Good! Now we can start looking for the stuff to make our face paint."

Jahrra returned their grins. "Perfect! Let me go fetch Phrym . . ."

* * *

As the three friends rode their horses in the direction of the Wreing Florenn, the forest that loomed just beyond the old ruin where Jahrra and Hroombra lived, they animatedly discussed the plan for the following day. Professor Tarnik, their stodgy, overbearing boor of a teacher, had decided to test their survival skills this year by pitting them against one another. Conquer the

Tales of Oescienne

Castle, a competition where the goal was to steal the banner from another team's camp while trying to protect your own, was his idea of examining how they would fare should they find themselves lost in the wilderness. Jahrra didn't think it was the best way to test their survival skills, but the anticipation of a good competition kept her silent on the matter.

"Why do we have to wear all white?" Gieaun complained as their horses kicked up dust from the road. "I don't look that great in white."

"Obviously so the dye will show up Gieaun!" Scede said, giving his sister a perturbed look.

They hadn't been given too many details about the rules of the game yet, but they had been told it would involve crossbows, soft-tipped arrows, dye pouches and white clothing. The class had already been divided into five teams of six, and they knew that they had the entire city of Aldehren as their battle ground, so long as they avoided the townspeople during their game.

"Like Eydeth and Ellysian would even notice a local shop owner if they tripped over him," Gieaun sniffed.

"They would if it made them easy targets," Scede countered with a mischievous grin.

That made Jahrra snicker, for there was nothing better, in her opinion, than having a good laugh at the twins' expense. Eydeth and Ellysian had been tormenting her since she was small and it had become second nature for her and her friends to blanch whenever their names were brought up.

Soon the three companions spotted a tangled bramble growing on the edge of the forest and all talk of the evil Resai twins and their unpleasantness was over. Jahrra climbed down from Phrym as soon as they reached the bramble patch and sighed with glee. The bushes were heavy with a dark purple berry.

Conquer the Castle

Archedenaeh, the enigmatic Mystic who lived in the center of the forest, had once shown these berries to Jahrra and her friends.

"They taste terrible," she had told them, "but they make an excellent dye for face paint if you mix them with white mud."

Jahrra, Gieaun and Scede had gathered some of the white mud near the creek the day before. Now all they had to do was mix in the right amount of berry juice to make the pasty paint the same violet shade as the banner they were charged to protect in tomorrow's grand battle.

"What should we paint on our faces?" Gieaun asked, wrinkling her nose at the dollop of purple mud on her fingers.

Jahrra grinned, and then proclaimed, "Dragons!"

* * *

By sunup the next morning, Jahrra, her friends, and all their classmates were crowded around the schoolhouse in Aldehren, patiently waiting for their teacher to show up and get the game started.

Kihna, Rhudedth and Pahrdh, the other three members of Jahrra's team, moved over to the edge of the crowd to join them.

"So, what did we decide to do for the war paint?" Pahrdh asked over his sister's head.

Rhudedth rolled her eyes at her brother and mouthed the word *boys* which resulted in a giggle from Gieaun and a snort from Jahrra. They quickly moved a few more feet away when someone from the green team glared at them.

"Dragons," Jahrra whispered quietly, pulling out a piece of worn parchment on which she'd sketched a design. "We decided to make it look like we were wearing masks."

Kihna peered over everyone's shoulder and arched a brow. Jahrra had drawn a crude face with two dragon wings covering the person's eyes like a mask. The dragon's neck curled onto the forehead and the tail trailed around one cheek and ended at the person's chin. Face paint wasn't necessary for the game of Conquer the Castle, but all six teammates had agreed it would be a nice touch.

"How are we going to paint that image on our faces?" Kihna asked when she was done studying the picture.

Jahrra grinned. "With this," she said, pulling out a jar of the dyed mud.

Fifteen minutes later, all six of them were sporting their dragon masks and Professor Tarnik was getting ready to read the rules. Several parent volunteers stood around him, holding canvass bags and small crossbows. As Tarnik cleared his throat, they started moving through the crowd of children, handing each one a crossbow and a bag full of arrows. Another adult had a sack full of paint packs for the soft-tipped missiles. When the team leader held up their banner, they were handed several of the paint packs in that flag's color.

"Hey Nesnan," Ellysian hissed in Jahrra's direction. "Nice outfit! Did the used clothing store give it to you for free because it was so out of date?"

This drew a few snickers and giggles from those nearest Ellysian, but Jahrra just ignored them. She knew they would make fun of her team 'uniform', but she didn't care. She was here to win the game, not compete for first prize in a fashion contest. Ellysian, of course, was wearing a brand new pair of fashionable white riding pants and a shirt and coat to match.

Jahrra sighed and waited patiently for their turn. The parent volunteers who were handing out their crossbows and arrows would also be monitoring the game; making sure all the rules were followed. Jahrra was grateful, for she knew of a certain set of twins that was prone to cheating in order to get their way.

Conquer the Castle

She gripped the wooden pole of her team's purple flag tightly. No one, especially not Eydeth and Ellysian, was going to capture her team's banner.

"You may place your flag anywhere within the boundaries of your marked territory," Tarnik called out in his sneering voice, "but it must be clearly visible from at least one location. The volunteers will be checking to make sure you follow the rules, so don't try anything sneaky."

Jahrra shot a glance at Eydeth and Ellysian and the smug looks on their faces waned just a little bit. Ellysian leaned in to whisper something in Eydeth's ear and his look turned even sourer.

Had her instincts been right? Had they been planning something? *Will be a bit hard now*, Jahrra thought with some satisfaction, *what with referees walking about to make sure all the rules are followed*.

"The points will be added up as follows: for each flag captured, the conquering team will receive fifty points," Tarnik continued. "For each spot of that team's color deposited on others, they will receive one point. For each spot of color deposited on you from another team, you will be deducted three points. Nothing above the shoulders will count."

Jahrra filed the information away. *Fifty points for each flag captured, one point for each time you hit someone, three points taken away for each time you are hit. Got it.*

Tarnik lowered the scroll he'd been reading from and scanned the crowd with his eyes. Jahrra could have sworn that he sneered when he spotted them, but soon he was done with his surveying.

"You will have five hours to defend your flag, capture those belonging to other teams, and to shoot any enemies. Flags, once stolen, can be hidden in plain sight on your territory, but they can also be recaptured and your own flag must always be visible. Your banner must be hidden within the area marked as your territory."

Jahrra listened intently as he explained that each team had a territory already marked with smaller ribbons to match the color of their flags; territories that they must find themselves. *This should be interesting,* she mused with anticipation. She delighted at the thought of the free-for-all that would ensue once everyone scrambled to find their territories while avoiding being shot by the enemy.

"Students, are you ready?" Tarnik shouted. "Remember, the winning team not only is assured full marks, but will also receive a full day off from school."

Everyone cheered, declaring that they were more than ready to begin. He reminded them once more to stay out of the way of the townspeople and to not wander any further than a hundred feet away from the edge of town.

With one last domineering look Tarnik shouted, "Let the games begin!"

Everyone bolted at once, shouting and scrambling to get to their respective territories, wherever they might be.

Jahrra and her team headed south, since it was the only direction no one else seemed to be heading.

"Might as well check in this direction first and avoid getting shot," Jahrra breathed as she and her friends jogged down the cobblestone road.

The town was still relatively quiet at this hour, but as the six friends scanned the side streets and patches of trees and bare hillsides for purple markers, the people that were out and about paused to watch their progress. Some even wished them luck in their game. Jahrra grinned. She hoped that their classmates' antics would prove entertaining for those who had to put up with their entire town being invaded.

Eventually, Pahrdh shouted, "There! A marker!"

Jahrra grinned as she spotted the violet ribbon dancing in the breeze. They had made the right decision in going south.

Soon, the six of them had established the edge of their territory. It included part of a city block and a sizeable amount of a small, forested hill rising up behind a row of buildings.

Jahrra held her hand to her eyes, squinting hard as she looked for a good location to place their flag.

"Let's see if we can find a place where we can blend in with the surroundings," she said.

"It's going to be impossible to blend in wearing white Jahrra," Gieaun pointed out.

Jahrra sighed in frustration. Gieaun was right and any minute the other teams were going to find an appropriate place to hide their flags and be on the hunt. Although their territory was large and there were plenty of suitable places to put their flag, Jahrra and her team were having trouble picking a good location.

"We need to hide it on high ground," Pahrdh insisted as they spun in circles in the middle of the street. "It will be easier to guard."

Jahrra shaded her eyes again and glanced between the buildings in the center of their marked territory. Her gaze trailed down the alley between two buildings, then up the leaf-littered hillside behind them. The buildings were the typical small business establishments found throughout Aldehren with the lower floor sporting a shop while the upper storey acted as the living quarters. A railed deck wrapped around both buildings, and trailing from the edge of the deck into two redwood trees on the hill was . . .

Jahrra grinned. "Perfect!" she cried.

Pahrdh and Scede turned to give her scathing looks. "Are you going to help us find a place to make camp or not?"

"Already found it. Look." She pointed up to the hillside and then to the lines running from the trees to the decks, the ropes sagging with the weight of freshly hung sheets and random articles of clothing, many of which were white.

"We can stake our flag between those two trees and two of us can sit in the branches closest to where the ropes are tethered."

Jahrra turned a mischievous grin onto her friends. "Everyone will just assume we are laundry."

"Excellent!" Pahrdh cried out with glee, already sprinting towards the alleyway, the violet banner flapping behind him.

The six of them quickly clambered up the hill and drove the flag pole into the ground. Jahrra ran back down onto the street to make sure the flag was visible enough to be seen by her classmates, then rejoined her friends on the hillside. From the center of the hilltop, they could just see over the rooftops of the buildings in front of them.

"Gieaun, you and Kihna stay here and guard our flag. Scede, you, Pahrdh, Rhudedth and I will split up and try to capture the others."

"Here," Pahrdh offered, pulling some of his own arrows out of his bag. "We were given a hundred arrows each, right? I don't think we'll need all of ours since we'll be trying to get in and out as fast as possible."

He pulled out a sizeable chunk, nearly two thirds of his supply. Scede, Rhudedth and Jahrra followed suit. Jahrra didn't sacrifice as many as the boys had; she had a special purpose for some of her own arrows.

Conquer the Castle

Gieaun nodded grimly and accepted the arrows and extra dye pouches from the boys, dividing them between her bag and Rhudedth's. Once they were well armed, Gieaun secured the bag of arrows and extra dye to her back, then turned and started climbing the tree, muttering protests as her hair got tangled in the redwood's needles. Kihna was already jogging to the other tree with her bag of ammunition.

"How's the view from up there ladies?" Scede called up to Kihna and his sister.

"I can see everything!" Kihna cried out.

"I just hope these crossbows have good range," Gieaun added. "If we can hit someone enough times, it should discourage them from making a run for our flag."

Jahrra nodded her head in agreement. Three points wasn't much, but multiply that by fifteen or even ten, capturing another team's flag might not garner enough points to win the game. Oh, and Jahrra was determined to win this one. Even more so, she was burning to capture the golden flag belonging to a certain set of twins and their team.

"Alright," Jahrra said, gathering her other three teammates around. "Scede, you're going for the red team, right?"

Scede nodded.

"Rhudedth, you're going for green and Pahrdh you wanted the blue team, correct?"

"Yes," Pahrdh said.

"And I'm going for the gold," Jahrra said with an air of vengeance.

"We wouldn't dream of taking that honor from you," Scede claimed, standing up straight and placing his closed fist over his heart in a gesture of obeisance.

Jahrra shoved him good-naturedly and in the next minute they were creeping down the hill to start the hunt.

"Be careful and good luck!" Jahrra called quietly to her teammates as they all took a different direction away from their base.

Although they had decided leaving two people behind to guard their 'castle' while the others used stealth and skill to sneak into the enemy camps was their best option, Jahrra felt nervous. She didn't think it would be the easiest way, but she was hopeful nonetheless.

Casting aside her wayward thoughts and sending up a plea to Ethöes that her friends fulfilled their own goals, she crept back through the city, staying close to the backs of the buildings and using the occasional wooded hillside to hide her progress. She had caught a glimpse of Eydeth and his team heading northeast when they had first dispersed, but Jahrra couldn't be sure that's where they'd find their territory. She decided that a surreptitious check of the city's perimeter would give her some answers.

She bristled in annoyance when the edge of her shirt snagged on a branch fifteen minutes later, drawing the attention of someone on the red team. She wasn't fast enough to dodge the arrow they sent her way and as she dove behind a tree, the tip of the arrow caught her hip. Gritting her teeth in annoyance, she moved quickly and silently further up the hill to get out of sight. She would have to be more careful in the future.

An hour passed before Jahrra finally caught a glimpse of something promising. She had descended back into the city, keeping to the shadows of the buildings. At one point she used a passing cart to disguise her movement, ducking behind it as it rolled past a clump of her classmates, all three of them armed with green-tipped arrows.

Conquer the Castle

She quickly ducked behind a building to wait for them to move on, but as she was waiting a splash of yellow caught her eye. Jahrra jerked her head to the left and spotted a yellow ribbon tacked to the corner of the building she was using for cover.

Feeling her heart leap into her throat, she swallowed hard and crept closer to the edge of the small shop. Another yellow strip of cloth was nailed to the corner of the city's stable several feet away.

Got you Eydeth, she thought as her eyes narrowed. Now, all she had to do was locate the flag without being seen . . .

Jahrra peeked around the corner of the building once more, and then she saw it. There was the golden flag she sought, waving gently in the breeze as if beckoning her forward. She was tempted just to run for it. Taking time to check the area for guards could draw their attention, but if she just bolted, maybe she could use the element of surprise.

Sweat dripped down her forehead and stung her eyes. She gritted her teeth. It was so tempting just to run . . . But she had already been shot at twice, hit once, and she couldn't risk acting before checking her surrounding area. *Patience,* she told herself, *patience* . . . Forcing herself to keep still, Jahrra carefully looked around the building again to assess her options.

Eydeth and his team had chosen well. Their flag, tied to a long, sturdy branch like all the other banners, was standing in the middle of an abandoned pasture behind the stables. Several rocks were piled up to keep the pole from falling over and most of the pasture was surrounded by a neglected yet sturdy fence.

Clever Eydeth, Jahrra mused wryly. Although the spare pasture was obviously not suitable to keep in horses, there was still plenty of good fencing to create an obstacle for anyone hoping to make a mad dash for the flag.

Jahrra narrowed her eyes and scanned the entire fence line. The most obvious entrance was several yards in front of her, where the gate had been left wide open. She spotted a few more gaps in the fence where a rail had fallen down, creating a hurdle. Those neglected areas wouldn't be as hard to get past as a solid fence, but it would be just enough to slow someone up and make them vulnerable for an ambush.

So, Jahrra thought as she finished her assessment, *you hope to lure us in and then trap us like sheep?* Jahrra would be very shocked if Eydeth and half of his team weren't currently hiding behind the thick shrubs just beside the open gate. Her suspicions were only confirmed when the tiniest rustle sounded from the bush closest to her. The leaves were thick enough to hide even the brilliant white Eydeth and his teammates wore, but Jahrra didn't need to see them to know they were there.

Now all she needed was a plan. Could she distract them somehow? If she had Scede, Rhudedth or Pahrdh with her, they might be able to pull it off. But her other friends were off trying to secure the flags belonging to the other teams.

I hope they aren't having the same trouble I am, she thought.

Minutes passed and no one from any of the other teams came by. Jahrra wondered if they were too intimidated to attack Eydeth's camp or if they were simply doing what she was doing: waiting and biding their time. Jahrra sighed quietly, her mind going back to the idea of making a run for it. She knew where Eydeth and his teammates were hiding, at least where some of them were hiding. She glanced back around the building. The shrubs were far enough away from the gate to prove a bit of a challenge if they were to try and shoot her from their hiding spots.

Should I trust my instincts? she wondered. *That they won't shoot until I'm clear through the gate? Could someone be waiting on the far side of*

Conquer the Castle

the field on the other side of the fence? Or will they just assume I'll run right in, not expecting an ambush?

Jahrra chewed at her nails and felt herself growing restless. *If I'm going to run for it, I had better have a plan of escape.* She eyed the wooded hillside beyond the pasture. If she could somehow grab the flag, leap the fence and make it into the trees, then she stood a chance. Jahrra studied the far end of the fence line one more time. There. A weakness. The top rail had come loose from one of the posts and was resting on the ground. She could hurdle that, easy. And if she just simply applied some of the skills she'd learn from her elfin trainers, Yaraa and Viornen, this should be a walk in the park . . . if her enemies were exactly where she thought they were.

It'll be risky, she told herself, taking a deep breath and getting ready to bolt, *but the reward will be so worth it.*

Jahrra stood up straight and took a deep, calming breath. She shoved the small crossbow into the quiver with the arrows and dye packs, tightened the straps, and shifted the bag so that it rested against her stomach and not her back. For what she planned to do, she needed her arms and back free. She took another deep breath, counted to three, and leapt into a full sprint. She quickly picked up speed, eating up the distance between the building she'd hidden behind and the wide open gate. Sixty yards, fifty, forty . . . She flashed through the gate, running at full speed and felt more than heard Eydeth and his comrades leap out of the bushes and run to close the gates.

Jahrra kept going, grinning to herself. She had been right. The flag was waiting for her, only twenty yards ahead now, in the middle of the pasture. A golden tipped arrow struck the ground just to the right of her, its yellow dye splattering harmlessly on the grass as her boots sped past.

Ten more yards . . . Another arrow chased her, this one landing between her feet, the dye just speckling her pants. *Not a true hit,* she thought to herself as she pumped her arms, her breath coming faster.

The flag was only a few yards away, but Jahrra didn't slow. She stopped moving her arms, but her legs kept up their speed. Just as she was about to pass the flag, she threw her arms forward, reaching out to grasp the wooden flag pole in one hand as she dived into a roll. Her fingers grasped the warm wood tightly as she tucked her shoulders and brought her head in to her chest. The back of her shoulders hit the ground with great force and the crossbow, in its bag with all the arrows, jostled about as she completed the roll, coming back up on her feet, her momentum barely changing. Without thinking, she tightened her grip on the flag, ripped free from its stone prison, and drove her legs even harder, aiming for the hole in the fence several yards ahead.

A few more arrows flew past her, one of them making a full strike in the low of her back. Cursing inwardly, she forced herself to speed up, this time zigzagging a little as she ran. *You can do this Jahrra! This is nothing compared to what Yaraa and Viornen make you do!*

She reached the fence, hurdled it with little effort, and continued sprinting up the rocky hillside, seeking the relative safety of the trees. Sweat poured down her face and her ribs ached from her hard landing, but she had Eydeth's flag and nothing was going to make her stop now. Just as she disappeared behind the first row of trees, she thought she heard the livid scream of her nemesis at the far end of the pasture. Jahrra allowed herself a small grin, but she didn't stop. She sprinted until she could hardly breathe anymore; moving deeper into the small copse but making sure she stayed within a hundred feet of the city's outskirts.

Conquer the Castle

After several minutes she slowed down and quickly stripped the yellow banner from its pole and tucked it into her bag before picking up her pace once again. This time she would make an extra effort at returning to her own camp unheard and unseen. The last thing she needed was to get ambushed by another team and earn enough dye stains to make her effort at capturing Eydeth's flag all for nothing.

* * *

Jahrra spent an hour of slow and careful weaving through Aldehren as she made her way back to Gieaun and Kihna. Despite her effort, she'd been shot by someone on the blue team as she moved from a forested hill onto the streets, and then had a near miss when she paused to adjust the bag that carried her ammunition. After the second shot she had slowed her progress down even more. *Won't do any good if I keep getting shot,* she grumbled to herself as she crept up to the boundary of her camp.

Before coming within range of the redwood trees, Jahrra cupped her hands and imitated the call of a mourning dove. Four more calls greeted her and she eagerly jogged the final incline to find Scede and Rhudedth leaning against the trunks of the redwoods, both speckled with their own collection of dye marks, but grinning foolishly.

"Oh no!" Jahrra breathed. "You guys were shot too?"

"Yeah," Rhudedth answered, "but we gave them back as much as they gave us, and look!"

She held up a green banner as her smile widened.

"Excellent!" Jahrra cried as she pulled Eydeth's yellow banner out of her bag.

"We managed to steal three flags!?" Scede added as he dropped the red banner on top of the others.

"And managed to keep ours safe!" Kihna said as she climbed down her tree to join them.

Gieaun was right behind her. "You should have seen all the people we shot!"

They all exchanged stories of their adventures for a few minutes, then Rhudedth looked up and said, "Where's Pahrdh?"

At that moment, another mourning dove call reached their ears and the five of them returned it, letting Pahrdh know it was safe to enter camp.

He looked rather glum when he climbed up to the top of their hill. He appeared to have more paint marks on him than everyone else and he didn't carry a blue banner in his hands.

"I was ambushed," he muttered irritably. "It was a trap. Ugh! I should have known!"

"It's okay Pahrdh," Jahrra said grinning. "We managed to get all our flags, so I'd say we've done better than expected."

"True," Gieaun added, "but the game's not over yet. Where are we going to put these other flags? We're allowed to hide them, but they have to be in plain sight. That's going to be hard to do, considering their colors."

Jahrra frowned, studying the green, red and yellow flags. Gieaun was right. They had at least a few more hours left in the game and any one of the teams they had robbed could descend upon their camp at any moment to get back their flag and to take off with the others if they wanted to. It was one thing to guard one flag, but with four, every team would be after them.

"No it won't," Kihna said confidently, responding to what Gieaun had said about hiding them. "Look."

She pointed over at one of the clotheslines that hung lower to the ground than the others. When they had first picked this spot as their camp, Jahrra had been slightly concerned that someone might trip over the line in the heat of battle, but had since dismissed it from her mind. Now, as she ran her eyes down the rope, taking note of the colorful sheets and towels that hung there, she grinned.

"Someday we're going to have to pay for all our good luck!" she cried as she picked up the pile of stolen banners.

The six of them spent the next several minutes arranging the stolen flags on the clothesline so that they blended in with the other towels, sheets and clothing. After that, they huddled around their own violet banner to discuss the plan for the rest of the day.

"I think we should be done with hunting for more banners," Pahrdh said with a hint of resignation.

"Agreed," said Rhudedth, "we should stay here and spread out, shooting anyone who comes within a hundred yards of our base camp."

Jahrra thought this was a good idea as well, but she feared Eydeth had something more sinister up his sleeve.

In the end, they went with Rhudedth's plan and for the next hour, they managed to scare off the other teams as they shot at them from the cover of the redwood trees and the height of the hill. When Eydeth and Ellysian failed to show up, Jahrra's nerves started to prickle. She called her teammates back down to talk it through.

"I know they are planning something," she said, her eyes scanning the shadows.

"Well, what do you propose we do?" Gieaun asked, crossing her arms and arching a brow. "Do you want us all to go out and spy?"

Jahrra opened her mouth to make a retort, but then she thought about Gieaun's words. "Not to spy," she said slowly, "but to lure."

"Huh?" Kihna asked.

"To lure!" Jahrra smiled mischievously and crossed her arms. "I have an idea . . ."

* * *

Jahrra was almost shot five more times as she crept back through the city, searching for any sign of Eydeth's team. *Curse them, where are they?!* Dread pooled in her stomach and sweat trickled down her back once again as she imagined that perhaps this had been their plan all along; to make her think they were plotting only to sneak into her camp while she went out looking for them. Jahrra was just about to turn back when an arrow whizzed by her head, a flash of yellow catching her attention as it disappeared into a pile of hay.

Mission accomplished! she thought as she sent a violet arrow towards one of Eydeth's teammates before turning and running directly back towards camp.

She was winded by the time she reached the top of their hill. She took a few moments to catch her breath before shouting, "Gieaun, Scede! Where are you guys?! Eydeth shot at me and I think he saw me come this way!"

She waited a few moments but was met with nothing but silence. She released a few curses then called out again, trudging back and forth between the redwoods, "Rhudedth, Pahrdh? Kihna? Where are you guys, you were supposed to stay and guard the flag!"

Jahrra turned to face the street below, one hand placed on her hip, the other letting her crossbow hang loosely at her side, as she donned a bewildered look. "Maybe they just left to scout the boundaries," she mused in a not-so-quiet voice.

Conquer the Castle

In the next moment something hard smacked Jahrra on the side of the face, causing her head to whip to the side and her vision to become clouded with stars. *What the . . . ?*

She quickly held her hand up to her temple and pulled it away to see if she was bleeding, but the moisture on her fingers wasn't red, it was yellow.

Hot anger welled up in her stomach as she snapped her head upwards. She scanned the bottom of the hill and was nearly hit again with another bolt. This one managed to graze her hair.

"What are you getting at Eydeth!?" she shouted angrily. "Head shots don't count you idiot!"

She moved herself more securely behind the redwood, willing the pounding in her head and the ache in her temple to go away. Her eye was watering and she was livid, but she had to control her temper or Eydeth would get what he wanted.

Eydeth casually stepped out from behind the building he was using as cover. Unfortunately, it would still be hard to get a clean shot at him. He held his crossbow loosely, another yellow-tipped arrow resting and ready to be fired.

"There's something nasty on your face and I was trying to kill it," he sniffed.

A torrent of chuckles answered him, all of them coming from the edges of Jahrra's territory.

She seethed in anger. There would most definitely be a bruise on her face tomorrow. *No Jahrra,* she thought as she ran the plan through her mind once more, *just have patience. Just get him and his cronies to move in a little closer . . .*

"Where are your worthless friends?" Eydeth asked. "I heard you calling out for them, but you got no answer. That was pretty stupid. Now do I not only know the location of your base camp, but I know that you have no backup either."

Despite his assurance that she was alone, Eydeth stepped carefully up the hillside, his head swiveling in every direction as he checked for an ambush.

Jahrra held her breath when he tried to peer into the redwood trees' branches, but when his gaze returned to her, she let it out slowly. He hadn't seen them . . .

"They didn't leave me here!" she answered haughtily, hoping that her irritation would lead his thoughts in another direction.

"Oh really? Then why were you so angry just a second ago when no one answered? Ha!"

Eydeth relaxed a fraction and Jahrra took advantage of his claim.

"No! They're hiding just a few feet away, waiting to attack you!"

Sometimes it was good to go with the truth, and this time it paid off. Eydeth threw his head back and laughed, lowering his weapon. "How could they be hiding? You can't blend in with a wooded hillside when you're wearing white with bright colors splattered all over it! We would have seen them by now!"

He turned his head and whistled. "You guys can come out, she's here by herself."

He turned back to face her, his eyes gleaming with malice as his sister and four of their friends stepped out from behind the buildings and climbed down from further up the hill.

"You're dead Nesnan," Eydeth breathed as he lifted his crossbow and took aim once again. His teammates followed suit.

"Oh, I don't think so . . ." Jahrra muttered under her breath. "NOW!" she shouted as she quickly threaded her crossbow through her arm and threw herself into a back handspring.

Conquer the Castle

All of a sudden, the hillside was alive with arrows, their purple and yellow dyed tips marking the ground, the trees, and anything else that got in the way. Jahrra managed to get to an oak tree just up the slope with only a few shots to the leg, but Eydeth and his team were faring far worse.

"Where are the arrows coming from?!" he screeched as he searched the trees once again, backing up to take refuge behind the buildings.

Jahrra managed to make it ten feet up into the tree before she stopped and pulled her crossbow off of her arm. She quickly readied an arrow and scanned the forest floor for possible targets, her grin growing wide when she noticed Ellysian retreating back up the hill. She was moving slowly, her eyes searching the redwood trees, so she didn't see Jahrra following her progress with her own weapon.

Ellysian's back was to Jahrra, so she took a breath, aimed for a spot between her shoulder blades and . . . lowered her aim to the middle of her back, her lower back . . . When the arrow was lined up with a spot just below Ellysian's tailbone, Jahrra released the arrow and relished the screech that ensued as the Resai girl went scrambling up the hillside, her backside splattered with dark purple paint. Two more purple smudges decorated her back before she found cover.

Remembering that they had a flag to defend, Jahrra whipped her head around and breathed a sigh of relief when she spotted the purple banner, standing proudly between the two redwoods. She had guessed correctly; their territory was too well defended for anyone to just run in and grab the flag. It wasn't worth the risk when six people were shooting at you from the trees.

"Retreat!" Eydeth screamed as he scrambled down the hill.

Jahrra caught one last glimpse of him before he rushed out onto the cobblestones below with his teammates. She laughed out loud when she counted the paint marks on his back. Plenty to put his team out of the running.

When they were certain that the enemy had fled their camp, the six friends climbed down from their respective hideouts: Gieaun, Kihna and Rhudedth from the redwoods and Pahrdh and Scede from the second storey porches of the closest buildings.

"That was fabulous!" Pahrdh proclaimed, throwing his arms in the air and giving Gieaun and his sister a hug.

Scede looked as if he wished to extend the same gesture towards Kihna, but before he could decide, she made the decision for him.

"You did so great!" she said as she stood on her tiptoes and kissed his cheek. "You shot everyone at least twice!"

Jahrra hid a grin as she watched her friend turn bright red.

Before any more celebrations could take place, the distant school bell began ringing.

Jahrra brightened immediately and glanced at all her grinning friends. "The game's over! Let's go see if we've won!"

The six of them gathered their own flag and carefully removed the other three from their hiding places and ventured back towards the schoolhouse. They walked confidently through the center of town, though they kept a wary eye out for people seeking revenge. Luckily, there were enough adult volunteers around to catch anyone trying to cheat.

The look on Eydeth's face when they finally all gathered in front of the schoolhouse was worth all the hard work Jahrra and her friends had exerted that day. When he saw them, he glared maliciously, but all Jahrra did was smile widely and flap out his banner as if she were taunting a bull. He crossed his arms and

Conquer the Castle

darted his eyes in another direction, his face turning dark red in anger.

It took Professor Tarnik and the adult volunteers a good twenty minutes to tally up all the points for each team. Jahrra patiently tolerated their examination, wondering if maybe she'd been hit more than she thought. The other teams, she had observed, looked just as messy as she and her friends did.

Finally, Tarnik had all the tallies and he was ready to proclaim a winner.

"In third place is the blue team. Although they lost their banner, they suffered the fewest wounds and were able to inflict enough on the other teams to earn a sizeable score."

Everyone clapped politely.

"In second place, the red team. They were able to successfully capture the blue team's banner and receive very few wounds as well."

The applause continued.

"And in first place, the team with the most points and the winners of a day off from school . . . the purple team!"

The clapping and cheering was louder this time, even though Eydeth's team didn't participate.

When everyone quieted down, Tarnik continued blandly, "Although they garnered the most wounds from other teams, they also inflicted the most onto others. And," he paused and gave Jahrra a suspicious glare, "they managed to keep their own flag and to capture three others. Congratulations."

Jahrra didn't think his best wishes were sincere, but she smiled anyways as she and her friends started making plans for their day off.

* * *

Tales of Oescienne

Hroombra glanced up from the manuscript he was reading when Jahrra clambered through the door. He was reclining at his great desk and had been waiting eagerly to hear how she and her friends had fared in their game, though one would not know it from his relaxed posture and calm gaze. It wasn't quite full dusk, but Jahrra started lighting candles anyways as she made her way across the room.

The dragon eyed her curiously as she approached. "I see you were hit," he mused, a grin tugging at the corners of his mouth.

Jahrra sighed, but threw a smile over her shoulder as she stretched to light one of the higher candles. "Yes, but not nearly as much as Eydeth was. And besides, my team won."

She beamed blissfully, recalling the events of the past several hours. Jahrra almost snorted at the sudden memory of hitting Ellysian right in the seat of her pants. Oh, what a glorious day it had been!

Jahrra finished with the candles and walked over to the great dragon, pulling up a chair and plopping down in it across the desk from him. She was exhausted, grimy and ready to fall asleep where she sat. She leaned back in her chair and held out her arm, examining the loose sleeve of her shirt. There were a few multi-colored stains there, but they had transferred themselves from her legs and torso. She knew she had at least three marks on her back, two on her stomach, one on her shoulder and hip, and several more on her legs. Yes, it had been a rather exhausting day.

Grinning, Jahrra leaned forward and stared at her guardian. He politely ignored her, his great amber eyes moving back and forth behind his spectacles as he read away.

Eventually, he took a patient breath and without looking up, he said, "Yes Jahrra?"

Conquer the Castle

"Aren't you going to tell me about the student that owned these clothes?" she asked with a grin, gesturing to the stained garments she wore. "If I recall correctly, we were interrupted the other morning when Gicaun and Scede came by."

Hroombra pressed his great hand against the scroll he was reading and looked up at her, brow arched. He took off his spectacles and placed them aside, giving her his full attention.

"What would you like to know?"

Jahrra's eyes grew wide. *Wait, he's actually going to tell me? Really?*

Jahrra choked on her words for a few moments as they tried to fight their way free. "Was he a noble?" she blurted.

Eyes glittering and his mouth quirked in a small smile, Hroombra nodded once.

"How old was he when he wore these?" she continued, pulling the dirty shirt away from her stomach.

"Oh, a little younger than you I believe, ten or eleven maybe."

Jahrra grinned. "Was he just as stubborn and determined as me?"

Hroombra gave a full smile, but Jahrra thought she saw a hint of sadness in his eyes.

"Oh, very much so Jahrra. In fact, you remind me so very much of him that I sometimes think I can see his presence in you somehow. It is impossible, I know, but that is the only way I can explain it."

Jahrra was about to ask what had happened to him, but thought better of it. Perhaps he had moved on when he was too old for a dragon mentor anymore. Or perhaps he had fled in fear when dragons were adopted as the enemy throughout their world.

Maybe, judging by her guardian's moment of sadness, something even more tragic had occurred.

Instead, Jahrra cleared her throat and went for a safer question, "Did he wear clothes like this every day?"

"Yes, actually. And sometimes every night."

Jahrra opened her mouth to ask something else, but tripped on her tongue when what Hroombra had said registered.

She switched questions. "What?"

Hroombra gestured at her outfit and said nonchalantly, "The garment you chose to wear as a shirt was his night robe and those, um, 'leggings' would be worn *under* a pair of trousers."

Jahrra merely stared at him and then her eyes grew wide and she felt the blood rushing to her face. She shot her hands to her mouth and said, "You mean I just spent the entire day traipsing through Aldehren in, in, some boy's *underwear!?*"

Hroombra merely grinned and said, "Afraid so."

Jahrra screeched and bolted from her chair, heading for her room. She didn't even hear Hroombra's chuckle trailing after her as he got back to his manuscript.

-The Spirit Stone Ring-

A rasping caw broke through the morning fog and the young woman sleeping in the small hollow jerked awake. It took her several minutes to remember where she was, for she had overused her special gift during the past several days and she wasn't at her best. The gift that made her a Mystic; a witness to the future.

She sat up slowly, rubbing her temples as she registered the familiar cold of fog and the rumble of the ocean far below her. No, she wasn't in her cave, tucked safely away in the Black Swamp in the middle of the Wreing Florenn, where no one would come and pester her. She had left that comfortable place just yesterday to follow her quarry, a Tanaan dragon and a human girl, as they fled north to the province of Felldreim.

Denaeh winced when her korehv, Mílíhn, let out another grumpy caw.

"Yes, yes, I know. You're hungry. Well, you had best start foraging on your own," she complained as she dug around in one of several pockets to be found on her blood-red cloak. "These bread crumbs won't last forever."

The large raven-like bird descended from his lookout in a flurry of deep blue, iridescent feathers to happily receive his breakfast.

As Mystic and bird shared their meager morning meal, Denaeh contemplated what her next move would be. Yes, she needed to head north to Lidien where she could keep an eye on Jahrra and her dragon protector, Raejaaxorix, but there was something she needed to do before she left Oescienne for good. Something she needed to know for certain before she got back to her scheming. She stood up, sending Mílíhn hopping off in agitation.

"Really, you ridiculous bird," she clucked at him. "You are spoiled rotten to the point of rudeness."

He merely hopped on top of a rock and fluffed his feathers at her.

"Now enough distractions," Denaeh said, taking a deep breath and reluctantly turning her head towards the sea far below her, "there is a delicate task that I must undertake."

The Mystic let out her breath and slowly made her way through the redwood grove until she came to a point where the land dropped off several feet below her. The cove was beautiful, even under the cover of fog, and the recent rains had fed the creek that now tumbled down to the beach in a magnificent ribbon of water. Denaeh glanced up to her left and followed the arm of land as it curved around the cove, its crest spiked with the same redwood trees she'd slept under the night before.

She didn't want to go down there; she didn't want to find what she already knew existed in a cave just to the south of this secluded cove.

"She could have been mistaken," the Mystic whispered as another wave rushed to the rocky shore. "It could be somebody else."

The Spirit Stone Ring

But Denaeh already knew, something that was intrinsic to being a Mystic, something that went deeper than instinct, yet she still doubted.

"I must," she murmured as she began to pick her way down the steep cliff side, "I must doubt, for I do not know how I'll accept it if it proves to be true."

Mílíhn left his rock and flew to the edge of the cliff, watching his master curiously as she made her way to the beach below.

The beach sand, more closely resembling tiny pebbles than miniscule grains, crunched under her feet and the icy salt spray of the sea tangled in her unusual, vibrant red hair. Denaeh merely pulled her cloak tighter.

"You really should take on your elderly guise old girl," she grumbled to herself. But that disguise only made her feel her age and she wanted to feel young for now, especially for what she would soon face.

Gritting her teeth against the cold and the flood of old memories, the Mystic slowly approached the waterfall, then followed the curve of the land towards the water once again. The tide was low and she thanked Ethöes for that particular blessing. Up ahead she found a network of caverns that meandered through the arm of land and opened up onto the other side, onto a cove no one else knew about.

"Well, not quite no one else," Denaeh mumbled as she picked the central cave and wound her way to the other side. "Jahrra and her friends managed to find it."

The air seemed cleaner once she came out into the dull light of the foggy sky once again, and as she clambered atop a solid shelf of rock riddled with tide pools, Mílíhn's harsh call from somewhere far above greeted her.

She smiled, knowing that he tracked her progress like a panther. "Silly creature indeed," she told no one in particular, "you'd think he was a hatchling newly fallen from the nest."

She also knew the bird could be quite a coward, especially when his master was in her current mood. He knew something was happening; that something significant had occurred in the past few days to make her withdraw into herself, he just didn't know what.

"Best stay up there Mílíhn!" she called as loudly as she dared.

The korehv returned a cry, this one signaling he would stay put and keep watch.

"Good," Denaeh sighed, standing up to her full height and pressing her hands to the small of her back.

"I guess I'm going to feel my age no matter how young I appear," she mused.

The Mystic simply stood there for several minutes, scanning the ocean, the beach and the cliff side with her strange topaz eyes. Eventually she found it, the cave that rested halfway up the cliff. Her stomach suddenly churned and her heartbeat sped up. She pulled her hands away from her back and held them out in front of her. They shook slightly.

Gritting her teeth and forcing her emotions to mind their own business, she climbed down from the rock shelf and alighted upon the pebbly beach. It took her five minutes to reach the base of the cliff and another five to climb to the cave's opening. It would have taken her far less time if her legs hadn't suddenly decided to turn weak on her or if her breathing hadn't abruptly become more labored. She didn't like these strange feelings; they were the same emotions she had learned to ignore long ago. Why did they have to come rushing back now? *You know why,* something deep in her mind told her. She brushed it aside and finished her climb.

As she stood on the small shelf in front of the cave entrance, Denaeh took a deep breath, and one last time, tried to bottle the years' worth of emotions that were trying so desperately to break free.

* * *

The first thing that hit her when she entered the cave was the smell, or the lack of smell. *If scent could be muffled, then this is what it would smell like*, she mused. The familiar odors of ocean, dust, pine and dankness were present, however. They were just subdued. It took a few minutes for her eyes to adjust to the darkness, but the beam of weak light pouring down from the ceiling helped. Stalagmites and stalactites decorated the cave, making it resemble the gaping maw of some hungry beast. The incessant drip of water hounded her ears, but the Mystic paid it no heed.

She glanced up, seeing a rocky shelf towards the back of the cave. She swallowed hard. "Please don't be who I think you are . . ." she murmured as she stepped forward, carefully avoiding a dark puddle.

Slowly, she made her way towards the rock shelf and once she reached it, she stood on tiptoes and peered over the edge. She pulled away quickly and blanched, her skin turning clammy and her head suddenly pounding. Yes, there was a body up there, but it was so far gone there was nothing to identify it; only the disintegrated remains of what had once been clothing and the skeleton that had once harbored a soul.

Denaeh wanted to leave it at that. "There is no way to identify you," she whispered harshly, her back to the rock shelf, her arms wrapped around her middle. "You have no mind left to search, and the one I seek has an even stronger mind than mine."

Then she said to the emptiness, "If you still lived somewhere in this great world, I wouldn't be surprised if you've shut me out for good."

But she had to make sure. She had to climb up there and see if there was anything left on this skeleton to tell her who he had been in life.

Taking several deep breaths, Denaeh turned around and climbed up to the shelf to join the long dead man. Something in the back of her mind told her just how gruesome this task was, but she ignored it.

The man's clothing seemed common enough, what little of it remained. His coat and pants might have once been blue, but they looked grey now. His boots, simple leather, were cracked and covered in a layer of dust. Denaeh carefully checked his pockets, the hairs on the back of her neck standing on end the entire time. She found a coin purse beside him, but it held nothing that might be familiar.

After several minutes, she sat back on her knees and took a deep breath. A flicker of hope danced in her heart like a new candle flame trying to avoid a breeze. "Perhaps you were wrong after all Jahrra."

Feeling far better than she had when she first arrived, Denaeh pressed a hand to the floor as she made to get up, but something caught her eye before she could. The dead man had one arm draped across his waist, but the other one lay loose at his side, the skeletal palm exposed to the ceiling. Something was there, in his palm.

Denaeh swallowed hard, the dryness of her mouth surprising her. Gently, carefully, she reached a finger forward and wiped the dust off of the object to expose the yellow shimmer of gold. No, the item wasn't in his palm, it was on his finger. A ring.

How she had missed it before, the Mystic couldn't say. She drew another deep breath and carefully slipped the ring from the skeletal finger, careful that she only removed the ring. Once it was free, it fell heavily into her palm, as if it had wanted to be there; as if it had finally been found by a long lost friend. Denaeh felt her heart clench and she mimicked the feeling by wrapping her fingers tightly around the ring. She couldn't look at it. She already knew what it was, but she didn't want to confirm it.

"Be brave now woman," she said breathlessly as she held the closed fist with the ring to her heart, "you must be brave."

Taking several steadying breaths, she lowered her hand and slowly opened it under the beam of light streaming from the ceiling. In her palm was a finely etched, golden ring, set with a beautiful stone. With her heart in her throat, Denaeh carefully turned the ring so that she could see the stone more carefully. It was like no other in the world, a pale crystal blue, almost clear, with just a touch of grey. And there, deep in the center of the stone, was a fleck of golden topaz. A spirit stone.

"Oh no," she rasped, swallowing the lump in her throat, "if you still lived, this would have found a way to get back to you long ago."

Denaeh enclosed her hand over the ring once again as an immeasurable pain suffused her heart. She barely remembered rocking onto her side as she held the ring close, for the darkness had fully taken over her.

Far above the cove a large bird sat in a redwood tree waiting for his master to return to him. A soul-deep, heart-wrenching wail echoed up from the cove, startling the bird. As he

Tales of Oescienne

resettled himself on the branch, he let out a long grumbling caw, a sound of lamentation to match the sorrow below him.

* * *

It was nearly sunset by the time Denaeh was done with her task. It had taken her nearly that long to pick herself up and accept the truth. The spirit stone ring had confirmed her worst suspicions; she knew it to be his. It would no longer seek him out, for he was no longer living for his spirit to call to it. She had known this, but it still raked at her heart. *You've been alone for so long old woman,* she told herself, *you'd think by now that you'd be used to that loneliness.*

The Mystic dug around in her pockets for the strongest piece of string she could find, a long, thin strip of leather. Carefully, she strung it through the ring, tied the ends, and placed the makeshift charm over her head. She would have preferred to wear the ring, but she knew as well as any that rings with spirit stones only accommodated the fingers of the one they were crafted for. Lastly, she tucked the ring under her collar so that it would rest safely against her skin, close to her heart.

Once she had finally recovered enough to drag herself out of her depression, Denaeh undertook the task of collecting the skeleton and bringing it down onto the beach in order to create a funeral pyre. It was hard work, climbing back and forth to make sure all the remains were accounted for while trying not to collapse under the weight of sorrow.

At some point in time, Mílíhn grew tired of waiting up in the trees. He flew down to join the Mystic, sitting on her shoulder and moving closer to her head. She found the gesture comforting and welcomed his company. His attention helped ease a little of the pain in her heart.

The Spirit Stone Ring

Finally, as the sun started to dip low in the ocean, Denaeh glanced woefully at the funeral pyre she had constructed. Using a dagger and some flint she kept to start her campfires, she set the dried seaweed and driftwood on fire, the flames slow to catch in the still damp air. The fog had long since crept back out to sea, and although she was sure it would return before daybreak, the Mystic was glad for a reprieve from its persistent drizzle. Stepping back, she watched as the fire spread, the heat of its presence not nearly generous enough to warm her chilled bones and hollow spirit. Mílíhn, still clutched to her shoulder, tightened his claws and grumbled into his wing, arguing with his own internal thoughts most likely. When Denaeh felt a gentle nibble at her ear, she smiled through her silent tears and reached up to stroke the bird's feathers.

"Thank you my friend," she whispered, her voice raw. "At least I still have you."

Mílíhn sighed as well, a small sound coming from his beak, and nestled closer to his master before tucking his head back under his feathers.

As the flames licked the air, Denaeh watched on. Her hand unconsciously moved and pressed itself against her heart, precisely where the ring lay, as tears streamed down her face. The sunset was a beautiful one, but the strange woman hardly noticed. Instead, she numbly turned away from the flames and headed back through the caverns to make her way up to her campsite from the night before. As she moved further and further away from the fire and smoke that was an acrid reminder of her loss, she was grateful for the pounding waves, for they masked the sobbing that had now taken over her body.

* * *

Tales of Oescienne

The snap of a breaking twig forced Denaeh to pause. Her eyes grew wide and she suddenly melted into the guise of an old woman, a trait unique only to herself and her sister Mystics. She and Mílíhn had been traveling well over two weeks now and they had only run into other people when they ventured into the small towns that dotted the coast. The Mystic had been keeping her gift of foresight reined in due to the energy it sometimes cost her, especially after her discovery at the coves. Now she let it unfurl, taking in all the living things in her current surroundings. *Foolish to have kept it in check,* she thought as goose bumps broke out over her skin.

She was traveling down an old, densely wooded trail somewhere between the coast and the great Thronn Forest in the northernmost part of Oescienne. In fact, she could see and hear the ocean pounding against the steep rocks several feet below her and the dark trees stretching on to her right were part of the thick wilderness she was trying to avoid.

The sound of movement caught her attention once again, and she quickly shuffled through all the harmless animals whose minds she'd invaded just seconds ago: a nervous squirrel, a pair of sparrows making a nest, a doe staying as still as possible, Mílíhn, several branches above her as he simultaneously kept watch and searched for food.

The loud crack of a much larger branch being snapped caused her to stop dead in her tracks. *Not keeping a close enough lookout, Mílíhn,* she thought acidly as she gritted her teeth, considering making her bird into a stew if she survived until nightfall.

She tried sending her awareness out again, but she only met the minds of simple creatures going about their business. And then . . . her strong, probing mind slammed against a wall so strong it nearly sent her reeling. Denaeh held her breath as the sudden pain in her head faded. There were people in this world strong enough to block the inquiring mind of a powerful Mystic, but they were few and far between.

Quietly and carefully, she reached up to press a gnarled hand against the spot where the spirit stone ring hung around her neck. "You were one of those people," she murmured with some sadness. "And if it wasn't for this ring you left behind, I would have still held out hope . . ."

At that moment, the shield that had been blocking Denaeh fell and a violent, powerful mind flooded her senses. She cried out at the sudden shock, throwing her arms up and dropping her walking stick as she tried to duck and protect her head as a large man came tearing out of hiding. He wasn't alone, but it was his mind that had created the mental block, one that had also hidden the five others that streamed out of the woods like a pack of wolves.

Oh no, Denaeh thought with dread.

They moved rather silently despite their crude armor and heavy footfalls.

"Restrain her," the one with the impenetrable mind growled.

Denaeh gasped as rough, strong hands grabbed her under her arms and jerked her up into a standing position. She thanked Ethöes she had had the sense to transform into her older form a few minutes ago. *Perhaps they'll leave an old, feeble woman alone . . .*

"Please," she said, trying to sound pathetic, "I'm just an old woman out for a walk."

"Is that so? Where is it that you live then?" the one with the powerful mind asked.

He had a calm voice, one that was too calm for Denaeh's liking. Its cold emptiness made her shiver.

"We saw no cabins or huts, and we've been scouting these woods for the last few days," another man answered, the one who had a vice-like grip on her right arm.

"She lies," said another from behind her. "Let us do away with her and move on."

The distinctive sound of steel being drawn forced Denaeh's heart to beat faster. She wasn't completely helpless; she still had plenty of tricks up her sleeve, but she really stood no chance against six men, one of them with a mind powerful enough to hide from her and shatter her own attempts at detecting it.

"Please kind sirs," she rasped, "I am a poor old widow, I have nothing and I won't be telling anyone of your passing."

There was a relative silence as the men's leader considered this. While she waited to hear her fate, she braved a glance up at him under her hood. He was tall and wore a hooded jacket himself, but the shadow of that cowl wasn't deep enough to hide the brand on one side of his face. Denaeh sucked in a harsh breath and felt her skin go white. The brand of the blood rose; Cierryon . . .

"Very well," the mercenary finally said, "search her for anything valuable and then set her free."

A rush of relief washed over her, but when the men started digging through the many pockets in her cloak, Denaeh began to protest.

"I have only herbs and small trinkets!" she cried, "Nothing of worth to men such as you!"

"This be a worthwhile trinket," one said as he fished her dagger out of her sleeve.

The Spirit Stone Ring

Another one ran his hand along her neck, searching for gold and silver chains. When his fingers grasped the leather string, Denaeh tried to curl up into a ball.

"No!" she cried, "Take the dagger, and I even have a few coins stowed away in a hidden pocket. Please, not that!"

But it was too late. The man had snapped the string and drew out the ring from underneath her shirt. His eyes lit up as he gazed at the gold band and unique stone.

"Now here's a treasure!" he proclaimed, licking his cracked lips.

Desperation and anger grew, and Denaeh spoke before thinking, her voice a threatening hiss, "You cannot take that!"

They couldn't take the spirit stone ring, it meant far too much to her. And she didn't think it had the power to return to her, the one whose blood had been shed to create it.

She imagined that if she had been in the guise of her younger self, with her full power free to do its will, she would have been quite formidable. But thank Ethöes above and below, she caught herself just in time. The Mystic bit her tongue as tears burned the corners of her eyes. *If they find out what you are, you will not survive long enough to regret your temper,* she told herself.

"Is it worth your life old woman?" someone asked gruffly.

Denaeh actually thought about it, but in the end she remembered there were more important things than trinkets, even trinkets that helped her hang onto the one good memory of her past. *It is almost worth that much,* she thought sadly, *almost . . .*

She slumped her shoulders and answered, her voice cracked and worn, "No."

The tight grip on her arms loosened a little. "You can have your dagger back old woman," one of the other men said, tossing the simple knife onto the ground. "This bauble should fetch a good price in the next town."

They chuckled and turned to leave, their leader snatching the ring from his fellow soldier and tucking it into a pocket in his jacket. The other two men let Denaeh crumple to the ground, laughing and making jokes as they left her there in the middle of the trail, an old helpless woman not to be feared.

How long she sat in the middle of the trail, the mud seeping into her skirts and cloak, Denaeh couldn't say. *They took it,* she thought morosely and bitterly, *they took the one thing I couldn't bear to part with.* Anger burned in her heart once again and if getting to Lidien wasn't so important, she would have followed those men and made them regret their mistake. But too much relied on her staying alive; she couldn't risk the possible consequences of taking on one of the Crimson King's branded servants and his soldiers.

"And no matter what I might tell them," she ground out, "they take orders from only one person."

Eventually, she dragged herself up using her discarded walking stick and wiped away what dirt she could. She simply leaned on the stick for several moments, trying to compose herself and to tell herself that it wasn't the end of the world that she'd lost the ring.

A wry, bitter smile crept onto her wrinkled face, her topaz eyes glittering with secrets that reached deeper than the roots of the ancient oaks surrounding her. *Oh no, it is an unfortunate loss, but you have lost far more than a simple ring.*

Mílíhn chose at that moment to descend from the safety of his perch. He landed on the ground in front of her, cackling and hopping around as if terribly distressed. Denaeh welcomed the distraction.

The Spirit Stone Ring

"So you have decided now to make your presence known? Coward! I could have used that sharp beak and grating voice of yours about twenty minutes ago!"

Despite her scolding, the Mystic was grateful for Mílíhn's presence.

She sighed and, casting her mind about once more to check if the soldiers had finally left, she melted into her youthful self once again.

"We need to be more vigilant if we are to make it all the way to Lidien, Mílíhn. Do you know who those men were?"

The korehv cocked his head to the side and exposed a curious, glossy eye. He puffed his throat out and growled low, took three hops, and leapt into the air, landing adroitly on the small branch that protruded from the top of Denaeh's walking stick.

She looked around hesitantly, even though she was certain the mercenaries had moved on. "They were Cierryon's henchmen and I fear they are looking for that girl of ours and her brooding dragon."

She sighed and absentmindedly scratched Mílíhn behind his neck. He grumbled and closed his eyes, enjoying the attention.

"We need to get to the City of Light as soon as we can."

Feeling a rush of renewed determination, Denaeh squared her shoulders and pressed on, pushing the ache of loss she felt for the ring to the back of her mind. As she picked her way over exposed tree roots and broken boulders along the rugged coast trail, she told Mílíhn that this time he needed to be a little more attentive because the next time they met strangers on the road, they might not be lucky enough to escape with their lives.

* * *

That evening, Denaeh set up camp amid a small rock outcropping that overlooked the sea on one side and the trail on the other. It was well secluded and an established fire ring told her that it was a popular spot for overnight camping.

I only hope no one decides to join me tonight . . .

The Mystic took off her crimson cloak and left it near the fire pit with her walking stick. She and Mílíhn spent the better part of the afternoon searching out firewood and something to eat for dinner. On her way out she set up a snare for rabbits, and was pleased to find she had caught something on the way back. Once she had a fire going and the rabbit skinned, the Mystic went about spitting it over the fire while the mushrooms she'd foraged earlier roasted near the coals.

The loss of the spirit stone ring weighed heavily on her mind now that she wasn't distracted with the business of putting distance between herself and the wayward soldiers, so she forced her thoughts to wander until they found a more suitable distraction. She glanced at her cloak, the hem of it drying with the heat of the fire, and grinned. The cloak had served her well on many occasions, despite its shocking red color. It held magic, a very ancient magic that she seldom called upon these days. As she considered its usefulness, an old memory broke free from all those jumbling about in her mind and floated to the surface. Her smile disappeared and her young brow furrowed. She sat up from her relaxed position and grasped the memory, letting herself think about it for a while.

Not really my memory at all, she mused.

A few years ago, she had tried to enter another person's dream without their permission. Such an action wasn't wholly unheard of, but it was considered a breach of etiquette in her line of business. She snorted at the thought. When she wanted information, she wasn't afraid to exercise all options, moral or immoral. *And I wanted to know your innermost thoughts . . .*

The Spirit Stone Ring

Denaeh smiled bitterly as she remembered. "But I still didn't learn what I wished to learn, now did I?" She placed her chin in her hand and stared at the fire as the wonderful aroma of roasting meat and mushrooms filled the air.

She added a log to the fire and watched as the sparks leapt to the sky. She had been after the identity of someone in the other person's dream; a figure who had visited the dreamer often. He always wore a green cloak, similar to her red one and he never spoke with the child he visited. There was a name for such recurring visitors to dreams: titles for what they symbolized. Soul Guardian, Dream Walker, Spirit Protector . . .

An old mantra danced through her mind then, one she had learned a very long time ago: *Soul Guardians represent someone known but not seen.* She couldn't remember exactly where she had heard it, but she had heard it often enough, repeated by those she knew and those who practiced magic, to have remembered it, even now after such people had long since disappeared from the world. She couldn't say if she truly believed it. It didn't make sense; someone known but not seen? It was just another riddle trying to explain a quandary.

But perhaps that was the point, she thought quietly, *like not appreciating someone in your life until they are gone.*

The Mystic shivered and instinctively reached for the spirit stone ring, but a well of bitter sadness bubbled up in her chest when she recalled that the ring was gone. She dashed a few tears from her eyes and took a heavy breath.

"Perhaps trying to think of other things was a bad idea after all Mílíhn."

The korehv, busy digging around in the leaf litter looking for grubs, paused long enough to grumble at his master and give her a quick look.

She grinned, despite her melancholy. It was a good thing she had Mílíhn, for making this journey alone would have been unbearable. *Especially after all I have learned.*

The sun still hadn't set by the time her dinner was done, but Denaeh was happy to call it an early night. Mílíhn finished off what she didn't eat; carrying the carcass off to the other side of the trail so any wild animals that might be drawn to it wouldn't find the campsite. Denaeh added a few more logs to the fire and bundled up in her now, mostly dry, cloak.

The sky was just growing dark when she was finally settled down. The familiar flap of wings greeted her and she turned her head to see Mílíhn perched just above her.

He stretched his wings and grumbled. Denaeh opened her eyes fully. She knew that sound.

"You want to go exploring? This late?"

The korehv repeated the sound and Denaeh sighed. "Very well, but don't wander too far and don't get caught away from the camp after dark. I expect you to stand guard tonight after your failure this morning."

Mílíhn grumbled his acquiescence and took off without a second glance.

"Odd bird. I've raised you from an egg and I still can't figure out how your mind works, even when I'm reading it."

Denaeh sighed, pushed away all of the ghosts that wished to torment her, and slowly fell into a dreamless sleep.

* * *

Denaeh came slowly awake the next morning, the rhythm of the pounding waves far below encouraging her to rise from her sleep. A bitter chill nipped at the air; the last remnants of the winter. The Mystic was reluctant to rise, for she felt warm under her cloak and the fire had burned out overnight. The few coals that did remain smoked like a sleeping dragon, reminding her of her need to get to the province of Felldreim as soon as possible.

Sighing deeply, Denaeh sat up and let her cloak fall away. She stretched and took a few moments to let her mind brush the furthest edges of the forest. Only small creatures stirring at this hour. She released a breath of relief, only to start at the pain that escaped with it. The soldiers were gone, and the spirit stone ring with them.

Denaeh got the fire going once again and managed to heat up some oatmeal in a small copper cup she'd pulled out from the folds of her cloak. *Where is Milíhn this morning?* she wondered. She hadn't heard him return last night and she had seen neither hide nor feather of him all morning. Usually he was up before her, pestering her for food or a scratch on the neck.

Just as she was beginning to worry, a flurry of dark feathers and a low caw greeted her as the wayward bird flew into camp.

"There you are! Have you been out all night?" The Mystic brushed the edge of his mind but didn't get an answer.

She stood and placed her hands on her hips. "Where did you go last evening?" she asked him, her young face smooth and serious.

He cawed and flicked his wings, as if asking for forgiveness. It was then that she saw something hanging from his mouth. Was it a piece of long hair? Twine?

Furrowing her brow, Denaeh moved closer, only to press her hands against her mouth to hide a gasp as her topaz eyes grew wide.

"Milíhn!" she cried, rushing over to him.

Carefully, she drew the item towards her. It was a long leather strap, knotted into a loop, and dangling at the bottom was . . .

"The spirit stone ring," she whispered, tears pooling in her eyes.

Mílíhn grumbled smugly, his version of saying *You're welcome.* He released his prize and watched with a glossy eye as his master settled the loop over her head and tucked the ring safely beneath her layers of clothing so that it could once again rest against her heart.

She turned to the korehv, her eyes still full of tears and said, "Thank you my friend."

Mílíhn simply ruffled his feathers, then shook, pleased at doing a good job.

"Well," Denaeh breathed, "if you stole this back, then they will eventually miss it."

She turned a wary eye on her bird. "Though I can count on you being very stealthy, I can't count on them dismissing the loss as a mere misplacement along the road. So, we had best get moving as soon as possible. The last thing we want is Cierryon's men after us."

Denaeh shuddered and quickly got to work dousing the fire and gathering her few belongings. As she got ready for traveling once again, Mílíhn helped himself to her leftover oatmeal.

Donning her cloak and deciding on traveling as an old woman for the time being, Denaeh stood up and called out to her friend. The dark bird gave an answering call as he picked his way through the canopy, acting as lookout as they traveled. The Mystic ambled along at a brisk pace, one hand clutching her walking stick, the other pressed against her heart where the spirit stone ring rested once more.

"Perhaps you did have enough magic in you to return to me after all," she whispered to the ring, wishing in her heart it was the ring's original owner that she spoke to.

The Spirit Stone Ring

A glow of joy, tiny but significant for its mere presence, spread throughout her spirit. The ring wouldn't heal her completely, but it would help. Facing the road and setting her sights on the future, Denaeh smiled brightly for the first time in what felt like ages.

-Fire and Ice-

Part One

The dragon Raejaaxorix reclined casually in his study, peering through the window that looked down over the city of Lidien. The morning was still very young and he knew he wouldn't be needed at Emehriel Hall for at least three more hours. For now, he would just enjoy the peace and quiet for once. He and a few of his fellow dragon friends had just returned from a long campaign in which they were required to spend countless hours in the air while checking the boundaries of Oescienne for trouble. They had not detected any enemies, so Jaax had given everyone some time off to rest before they began the same routine again.

Jaax sighed, the air around him heating up with the fire that smoldered within him. It was a tedious job, guarding the young girl Jahrra from a distance, but it had to be done. Luckily, none of his companions ever complained, well, almost none of them. Jaax quirked a knowing grin at a faded memory: Shiroxx, a Tanaan dragon like him, constantly asking why they had to scour the fringes of Oescienne, hoping to spot danger when it would be so much easier just to bring the child to Lidien where the Coalition could watch her from its door step.

Oh Shiroxx, Jaax thought now, *you just don't understand.* He glanced out of his window once more as the rising sun transformed Lidien from a pale chalk color to the pinks and golds

Fire and Ice

of the rose granite that had been used to construct most of its buildings. *Lidien is such a large, busy place, Jahrra would have surely become lost here.*

The girl was in the care of his dear friend and old mentor Hroombramantu, a Korli dragon who had survived many a turmoil and several decades in Ethöes. Hroombra, the founder of the Coalition for Ethöes, an elite group of dragons, elves and other beings intent on returning the world to its former, peaceful self, had established Jaax as the group's leader several years ago and now lived quietly in the south of Oescienne. And with him lived Jahrra.

Jaax took another deep breath and considered the paperwork on his desk. Many of the letters were from Hroombra, informing him of Jahrra's progress. He smiled fully when the old dragon described how much the girl loved her semequin, Phrym, and how the young horse was helping her through a recent and painful loss.

Before the dragon could let his mind dwell on the current tragedy in Jahrra's life, a soft but assertive knock came from his study door.

"Master Jaax?" a feminine voice called out.

Jaax took a breath, pushed the letters aside and said, "Come in Neira."

A Nesnan woman, not quite middle aged, with brown hair and a calmness to her demeanor, pushed the great wooden door open and stood just inside the study. She clutched what appeared to be a sealed document in her hands and she had a look of worry on her face.

"What is it?" Jaax asked his house maid, his attention now fully on her.

"This was just delivered from a courier. He said it was for the head of the Coalition in Lidien." She swallowed and took a breath. "He said it was urgent."

Jaax rose and crossed the room, his great tail sweeping behind him and his wings tucked snuggly against his back.

"Thank you Neira," he said succinctly, taking the rather large missive she offered him in one clawed hand.

Neira nodded and left the room to get back to her own work. Jaax severely hoped that she was making a big pot of strong tea, for he suspected he would need it. He moved back behind the desk and sat down once again, cracking the scarlet wax seal with one claw. His emerald eyes darted across the paper, his heart sinking with every word. When he was finished, he raised his head and stared at the far door for a moment, then turned his eyes on the huge map that took up most of one wall. It was one of the most detailed maps of Ethöes in the province of Felldreim, and he had paid the artist well to paint it upon his wall.

He scanned the province of Oescienne, its northern border just south of Felldreim. He noted Lidien on the map, resting near the coast and perched above the mouth of the great Saem River. From there he let his eyes wander northeast across the Great Hrunahn Mountains, over the Hrwyndess River and across the great channel that separated the island province of Yddian from the rest of Ethöes. There, on the southern tip of the island and nestled in the foothills of the Krehken Mountains, lay the city of Ahseína, a relatively small community that made its livelihood mostly by raising sheep for wool and fishing when the sea wasn't rough.

Jaax closed his eyes and sucked in a deep breath through his nostrils. *A small, unthreatening community with a very big problem.* Jaax returned to his desk and scanned the letter again. It was from

Fire and Ice

the town's patron, a wealthy landlord who collected taxes and protected the people when they were troubled by wild creatures or outsiders who wished to cause harm. But he couldn't protect them from this newest threat: a dragon. And not just any dragon, a Morli dragon.

Jaax forced his deep breath back through his nose, singing the air with hot smoke in the process. One of the Crimson King's war beasts had broken loose, so it would seem, and had crossed the channel seeking its freedom. Jaax had no doubt that the plentiful herds of sheep dotting the hillsides of southern Yddian tempted the beast, but it wasn't the citizens of Ahseína's fault that their way of life was so appealing to the monster.

Yes, Jaax thought with angry bitterness, *dragon or not, you are a monster.* The Morli weren't like the other dragons of Ethöes. They had been specially selected and developed by the Tyrant using dark magic and the cruel enslavement of existing dragons. The Morli were mindless, vicious monsters that knew one purpose and one purpose only: to destroy anyone and anything that opposed the rule of the Crimson King, the tyrant of the east.

Jaax's earlier relief at not discovering the Tyrant King's men sniffing around the borders of Oescienne disappeared in a snap. He would have to do something about this renegade dragon, and he would need to do something fast before Ahseína was destroyed and the monster turned its wrathful gaze upon another city.

* * *

Essyel Auditorium was alive with the rumble of over a hundred voices, male and female alike, as the various members of the Coalition of Ethöes argued amongst themselves over the news their leader had just shared with them.

Jaax pinched the bridge of his very long snout and half closed his eyes. He was getting a headache and Neira's famous tea had not been strong enough to ease his nerves completely. Shortly after reading the letter from Yddian and mulling it over for several minutes, he had called his house maid back to have a message delivered to all the members of the Coalition currently present in the city. They were to meet immediately, earlier than their usual time, to discuss a matter of great importance. That had been an hour or so ago, and as soon as Jaax had read the letter aloud to the entire hall, the arguing had broken out.

"This is getting us nowhere," Dathian commented next to him. He had to shout to be heard.

Jaax forgot the irritating headache and eyed the young elfin prince. He had arrived only a few short months ago, the youngest son of a royal line in Dhonoara who wished to become a scholar and not a monarch. The Tanaan dragon had liked him right away, what with his careful ways and quiet, but friendly demeanor. Dathian's father had allowed him to reside in Lidien in order to study, but if and only if he agreed to represent his royal family in the Coalition for Ethöes.

"You are right," Jaax answered. He cleared his throat and let out a burst of blue-green flame to get the hall's attention. He tried not to grin when everyone stopped dead in their conversations, eyes blinking wildly at the pyrotechnic display.

"Let's approach this issue in a more orderly fashion," Jaax said.

Someone towards the top of the room stood and called out, "Lord Jaax! Shouldn't we consider the possibility that this dragon has been sent by the Crimson King as a preemptive strike against his enemies?"

Fire and Ice

Oh blessed Ethöes, please no . . . Jaax thought as his stomach twisted.

The light murmur almost grew to an intolerable level again, but Jaax raised a great hand and said, "I can't say that that isn't a possibility, but since the message claimed it was only one dragon that has been attacking the town, I remain optimistic."

"How can you remain optimistic when one of the Tyrant's battle dragons is wreaking havoc upon innocents?"

The question, coming from a Resai man somewhere in the center of the auditorium, was greeted with shouts of compliance.

Jaax sighed again and answered before the room could become lost in argument once more, "I am not insinuating that this situation isn't serious, and something must be done to stop the attacks."

He cast his gaze up the rows of chairs, towards the back of the room, and caught the eyes of a familiar red Tanaan dragon. Shiroxx stood quietly, Sapheramin and Tollorias, two Korli dragons, on either side of her. The two Korli were on leave from their duties to the Creecemind king in Nimbronia, but would need to be returning there soon. The three of them were the only other dragons in Lidien at the time, and Jaax was going to ask them an enormous favor. He grimaced, but it was the only way.

Taking a steadying breath, he said loud enough for all to hear, "Sapheramin, Tollorias, Shiroxx," he looked at them each in turn, "I have a plan, but I'm going to need your help."

They already knew what he was thinking, for the two Korli adopted grim looks on their faces, whereas Shiroxx's eyes seemed to glint with excitement.

Jaax felt his mouth twitch with a half grin. *Yes, you do love a good fight Shiroxx,* he mused.

"So what is this plan?" a woman dressed in an opulent dress called out.

Raejaaxorix waited for the murmuring to cease. Then casting one more glance at his fellow dragons and arching an eyebrow at the young elfin prince next to him, he cleared his throat. "I propose that my three dragon companions and I fly to Ahseína and destroy the Morli threat. Immediately."

* * *

Early the next morning Jaax and his three dragon companions left Lidien, flying northeast towards the island province of Yddian. He led the quartet while Tollorias loomed like a large, dark grey thunderhead just beyond his left shoulder. Sapheramin, her pale cobalt scales matching the cloudy sky, situated herself somewhere behind him and to his right. Shiroxx was nothing more than a red blot trailing far behind them, watching their backs.

They made it as far as the eastern edge of the Great Hrunahn Mountains late into the next evening, making camp on a high mountain ledge as a storm threatened overhead.

"It looks like it's heading east," Sapheramin noted balefully.

Jaax nodded soberly. It seemed the tumultuous weather would follow them on their journey.

By the next morning the clouds had thickened, but they were not yet ready to release the rain they carried. The four dragons pressed on, cutting over the Hrwyndess River and the beautiful countryside of eastern Felldreim. They camped earlier the next evening, on the rugged coast of southern Rhohwynd.

"The weather over the channel can change in a heartbeat," Jaax told his friends as he gazed out across the choppy sea.

The clouds still drifted overhead, but the wind could pick up at any moment and he wanted everyone to be as well rested as

Fire and Ice

possible when they reached Ahseína on the other side of the water. *We don't know what awaits us there.* He shivered when he remembered one of the concerns of the Coalition members. What if this was a trap?

Jaax gritted his back teeth. *No, it couldn't be a trap.* The Crimson King, if he were intent on starting a war, would do so with a far greater degree of fanfare than baiting a troupe of dragons into assisting a seemingly insignificant town. Jaax chuckled bitterly. *No, he would be sure to draw the most attention possible.*

Shiroxx eyed him warily, but he merely gave her a smile he hoped was encouraging and said, "We fly before dawn."

* * *

The clouds had thickened by sunup, and the dragons were only a few miles into their trek across the wide channel when the clouds finally opened up. By the time they spotted the coast of Yddian in the distance, the rain and sleet had been pelting them for nearly an hour. They passed over rocky shores and conifer forests, foothills and the lower peaks of a mountain range before the town of Ahseína crawled into view. It was a sprawling settlement, wedged between the sea and the foothills. Great pastures partly full of multi-colored sheep surrounded the archaic buildings and a small castle, presumably belonging to the patron of the town, or so Jaax assumed, perched on the lowest hill closest to the town. Just to the east of it, on another low hill, was a giant wooden barn that looked like it could fit a whole kruel of dragons.

Shiroxx beat her wings and drew close enough to Jaax to speak to him. "I think we are just in time. Look."

She gestured off to the south and Jaax's stomach did a flip. A huge, dark red beast appeared to be rising from the ocean itself. Its massive wings easily took up half the town, and its grotesque head and mouth displayed an impressive amount of jagged teeth, many of which protruded from its lower jaw. It only had two legs and a long, powerful tail with spikes running down its ridge.

Jaax blanched when the creature opened its mouth and let out a terrifying roar. Even from his height, he could hear the screams of the townsfolk far below. He gave them a quick look as they scattered, running to the closest buildings. When the creature drew breath and spit fire upon the closest wooden house, Jaax felt his skin crawl beneath his scales.

"Quickly!" he bellowed. "We must stop it before it burns down the entire town!"

The four dragons split from one another, working to encircle their common enemy. Sapheramin and Tollorias breathed their red fire while Jaax and Shiroxx breathed the green-blue flames that were a trademark to their particular kruel of dragons. Their plan was working; they had distracted the Morli from its attack.

Jaax took this small opportunity to dive from the sky, landing in the center of town in order to quickly assess what damage had already been done and to see if he could reassure the townsfolk that help had finally arrived. Luckily, the creature hadn't set anything on fire, yet. Some of the townspeople were still running around, terrified, but one man dressed in the fine clothes of a noble came running up to Jaax.

"Are you from Lidien!?" he asked frantically.

"Yes," Jaax said, keeping his eye on his comrades and the dragon they kept at bay.

"Please, help us! Don't let that thing kill any more of our people!"

Jaax drew himself up as he began flapping his wings once again. "I won't. I promise."

Fire and Ice

He didn't stay to find out what else the man had to stay and was soon flying high above the city, moving towards the three other dragons.

"Let's drive him out over the channel," Jaax called out to his companions. Their nods of affirmation were his only sign that they had heard him.

They quickly formed a half circle and began driving the Morli back towards the water with their fire. The stubborn monster put up a hard fight as he returned their fire with his own. It was tedious work, trying to get the beast to move while not getting singed themselves. Once the monster was over the water, Jaax and Tollorias held their positions while Sapheramin and Shiroxx took to flying in, fast and close, to hit it with their fire and sometimes their claws or tails.

The battle went on this way for nearly an hour and the icy rain and wind that had followed them to Ahseína didn't help the situation. Its persistence caused Jaax's wings to ache, but he pressed on with his friends as they battled the massive Morli dragon. The creature was beginning to tire, he could tell, but then again, so were they. Shiroxx dove like a red lightning bolt, swiping her claws at the monster's wings. It screamed, the roar of its fury blending with the roll of thunder.

Jaax couldn't even see Sapheramin and Tollorias any longer, their grey and blue colors blending too well with the cloudy sky. He drew in a breath and flew straight towards the Morli dragon, releasing a burst of green-blue flame as he passed under it.

The monster bellowed again, but instead of inching back like it had done earlier, it turned and started heading east. Then slowly it banked its wings, as if to turn around so it could come at them again.

Jaax flew to join Shiroxx and the two Korli dragons already hovering far above the channel.

"What is it doing?" Jaax roared over the combined sound of dragons' wings, churning waves and howling wind. "Is it coming back for a fresh attack?"

"I don't know!" Tollorias answered. "It shouldn't have any strength left! We've been at it for a good hour!"

Jaax gritted his teeth and watched the creature carefully, its dark red color almost impossible to track. Then, with a sinking feeling in his stomach, he yelled, "It's not coming for us! It's headed back to Ahseína!"

And if to prove his point, the creature made a sharp dive towards the small town, releasing an orange torrent of fire.

Jaax's heart dropped. *No!* he thought, *I promised!*

"Quickly!" Tollorias screamed as he dove, heading straight towards the distant shoreline. The other three dragons were right on his heels.

By the time they reached Ahseína, a fire had taken hold of most of the buildings in town, despite the rain. A hot anger burned through Jaax as he made a mad dash at the giant dragon hovering lazily over the edge of the city that had not yet caught flame. Its wings were torn and its wing beats were sluggish.

Good, Jaax thought with some satisfaction, *at least we've nearly ended you.*

The monster turned its head then, its saber-like teeth protruding far from its lower jaw. It saw Jaax, then opened its mouth and turned towards the people running for cover just below it. Jaax looked too, and he felt his scales lose their color. A girl came tearing out of one of the burning buildings, screaming and falling to the ground as one side of her body burned with flames. She managed to get most of the fire out when she stumbled into a puddle, and Jaax secretly thanked Ethöes for the rain that had hindered them earlier.

The Morli dragon became distracted from the other people and focused instead on the girl, now curled into a ball and whimpering on the cold cobblestones of the street. In that instant Jaax anticipated what was going to happen. He let out a frustrated growl and beat his great wings, picking up speed as he flew directly towards the other dragon. The creature had opened its mouth further in order to finish what it had started with the girl, but Jaax, never slowing his flight, crashed into the monster, grabbing onto its lower jaw and scraping at the exposed stomach with his clawed feet.

Although the Morli was almost twice Jaax's size, the force of his attack caused the two of them to tumble in the air and crash into a few ruined buildings on the other side of the street. Jaax grunted with the force of their landing and then sucked in a sharp breath as something crushed one of his fingers. He dared to take a quick look at it and realized that during the fall one of his hands had remained grasping the Morli's jaw, with the middle finger not safely placed between the monster's teeth like the others.

Jaax clenched his teeth as he removed his damaged hand when the beast opened its mouth to draw breath. The pain was far worse than he thought possible, so he drew his arm into his chest and flapped his wings to get away from the dangerous dragon that still struggled to get up. Luckily, the Morli had landed first and had received the brunt of the fall, but it was still alive and looked even angrier than ever.

"To me, Jaax!" Shiroxx called from above.

Jaax glanced over his shoulder and spotted his companions. With much effort he managed to join them in the sky, his bruises and broken finger forgotten for the time being.

"Let's end this," Sapheramin hissed, her blue eyes hard with anger.

Jaax nodded grimly, trying to stay airborne as his head swam from the pain of the fight.

Together, they descended so that they flew directly over the fallen threat, the Morli dragon finally showing signs of defeat. On Jaax's signal, the four dragons released their fire, killing the Morli dragon before it had a chance to recover. Its screams of pain and anger filled the ruined town, and when the job was finally done, the silence that swept over them was chilling.

Eventually, the four dragons landed exhaustedly in the middle of the street, the soft patter of rain welcome to their ears. They approached the fallen enemy carefully, its charred carcass hissing as the icy raindrops fell upon it.

"It's dead," Tollorias said grimly as he nudged the creature's lifeless leg.

Jaax limped over to see for himself and Shiroxx eyed him carefully.

"Are you alright?" she asked.

Jaax snorted. "I got my hand caught in its mouth when we tumbled from the sky."

"It looks pretty bad," Sapheramin commented, her brow furrowed. "I think it's shattered."

Jaax gritted his teeth and hobbled forward, still clutching his arm in close. He *knew* it was shattered. He had felt the bone splinter himself. A wave of nausea hit him at the memory and he staggered.

"Steady old friend," Tollorias said with a grin.

That only made Jaax grit his teeth even more.

Eventually, the townsfolk emerged from their hiding places to cautiously approach their fallen enemy. When they saw that the

Fire and Ice

Morli dragon was truly dead, they all began cheering and dancing in celebration. The rain continued, but they all started making their way towards the large barn that stood upon one of the low hills just outside the city limits.

"That accursed slave of Cierryon didn't manage to burn our storage barn. Hah!" the town's patron lord crowed as he led his shaken, but gleeful people up a well-used trail.

Jaax and his dragon friends straggled behind, especially Jaax with his broken finger, as everyone piled into the massive building, gathered wood in the hearths, and got several fires going, with the help of their dragon saviors of course. Many of the mixed Resai, Nesnan and elfin men and women pulled out flutes and pipes and started playing lively music.

The building was truly a sight to behold and large enough to hold the four dragons easily with all the townsfolk, but Jaax stayed close to the entrance and watched the revelry unfold in front of him.

"Come in Jaax! It is much warmer in here than hovering near the door," Shiroxx said, her head held high and her brown eyes gleaming.

Jaax smiled but shook his head. "I'm more comfortable here," he insisted.

The red Tanaan dragon merely shrugged and turned to talk with Tollorias about something.

"What is it Jaax?"

Jaax started and accidentally put weight on his injured hand. He turned to see Sapheramin's kind face.

"Nothing," he answered, pulling his hand in close again.

"Now, don't give me that, I know your looks," she answered. "Something is bothering you."

Yes, something was bothering him, and not just his broken finger. He didn't want to talk about it and ruin the current mood, but Sapheramin's persistent presence finally pulled it out of him.

"I cannot understand why they celebrate so," he admitted, a tinge of guilt peppering his words. "Their entire village was nearly destroyed and some of their people lost." He turned his eyes on Sapheramin. "I almost witnessed a girl nearly burn to death."

The Korli dragon nodded once, her eyes dropping to the ground. "It isn't your fault Jaax," she murmured sincerely.

He clenched his jaw then said, "I promised their patron. I gave him my word."

"And you fulfilled that promise!" she hissed. "You, *we*, brought down that Morli dragon and took away the threat to their village and livelihoods."

"Yes," Jaax laughed bitterly, "not before it burned down half of their homes and killed a good number of their people."

"Lives are always lost in battle Jaax; that is the way of the world. You know this. I do not like it any more than you do. All we can hope to promise is that we do our best to end such atrocities when we can. No one can ask any more of us, or expect any more either."

Jaax took in a slow breath and stared at the floor. She was right. He knew she was right. But that didn't take away the feeling of failure that engulfed him. If anything, only time could do that.

Fortunately, Jaax didn't have much longer to focus on his dark thoughts, because in the next moment a woman broke into their conversation.

"Pardon me, but are you the dragon with the broken finger?"

Fire and Ice

Jaax glanced up to find a pair of dark eyes framed by a flurry of white hair gazing sharply back at him. The woman looked Nesnan, maybe Resai, and she stood with a sturdy confidence that only a healer could pull off. The bag of herbs and salves she carried with her only proved his suspicions to be correct.

He gave Sapheramin a knowing look, but the Korli dragon only grinned and bowed her head before moving back into the crowd of celebrating townsfolk.

"Let's see that finger," the healer said, rummaging through her pouch for supplies.

Jaax sighed and decided to cooperate. His finger was broken after all, and it would do no good to delay healing it.

The woman pulled out a large jar of salve and set it aside. Jaax offered his injured hand and the woman eyed it with her chin in her hand. She clucked her tongue after a few moments. "Lucky that demon didn't take the whole finger."

"Lucky he didn't take my whole hand," Jaax countered.

The healer beamed, her eyes dancing with mischief, and then she sobered up. "I should be able to mend it, but you'll have to keep it wrapped against another finger for several weeks until the bone knits. I'm afraid this scale will eventually fall off."

She reached out and tapped Jaax's injured finger, just above the knuckle, where one of his scales appeared to be slightly out of line with the others. He hissed and drew his hand back from the sharp pain her action had caused.

She only chuckled and started unscrewing the lid from her jar.

A true healer indeed! Jaax thought grouchily. *All healers love to prod at your sore spots.*

Tales of Oescienne

The woman turned back around, her hands lathered up with the strange ointment. "I promise to be gentle," she said, holding up her right hand when Jaax gave her a dangerous look.

Reluctantly, he held out his injured finger and she carefully smoothed the salve over it. He only winced twice.

"What does that do?" he asked when she was done. He sniffed at it. It smelled like strong mint.

"It will help numb it as I encourage the pieces of bone to settle back together."

Jaax raised his eyebrows at that. "So you have the gift of magic as well?"

She gave a full smile, her eyes glittering with calm pride. "Ethöes has blessed me well, dragon friend. I have helped many with it."

The process of aligning the shards of bone in his finger required the healer to close her eyes, rest her hands over his injury, and hum a tune that seemed as old as the earth itself. Jaax didn't feel any pain during the whole process, only a strange tingling sensation along his middle finger.

"There," the woman said after a few minutes, "done. Now, if you keep it bound to your other finger, it should heal well."

She finished up by wrapping the newly tended digit to the one next to it.

"You should also keep as much weight off of it as possible," she added. "At least until it no longer aches when you put pressure on it."

"Thank you," Jaax began, and then looked at her questioningly.

"Faerra," she offered.

"Thank you Healer Faerra, I shall take your advice to heart."

Fire and Ice

"And thank you dragon friend, Raejaaxorix, for what you have done for our village."

She nodded politely, packed her bag, and disappeared among the revelers to seek out the others who had been injured during the battle. Jaax watched her go, wondering if Sapheramin had given her his name and hoping she tended to the girl who had been burned. He lifted his hand and looked at the finger, now tightly bound to its neighbor. The salve was wearing off and the dull ache was returning, but it didn't feel so out of place any longer.

Sighing, he sought out his companions. They were at the opposite end of the great barn, so he braved the dancing and laughing men and women to reach them.

"I'm going to find a place where I can get some sleep," he told Tollorias. "It would be best if we left tomorrow, sometime in the morning."

Tollorias nodded and Jaax left him and the other two dragons to enjoy the festivities. It was still raining when he stepped out into the open hillside, but as he climbed further into the hills, he found an empty hollow that was covered with tall, dense pine trees. Jaax curled up on the thick matt of evergreen needles and willed himself to sleep. He was exhausted, but the image of the girl half on fire haunted him, and it was a long time before he was safe in the realm of dreams.

* * *

The rain had gone by the next morning, but a heavy fog clung to the mainland and disappeared out over the sea. Jaax had risen early, fighting the nightmares that often visited him after he had taken part in any violence. He met the other dragons in the center of town, the two Korli and Tanaan bidding farewell to those townspeople who had been spared the Morli's wrath. Only a dozen or so people had lost their lives to the creature, a small number considering the size of the town and the damage that had been inflicted, but to Jaax it had been too many.

If we had come sooner, if I had not backed off on the dragon before it had a chance to return to town . . . Jaax shook his pounding head and lifted his hand to rub his scaly face, only to wince when the movement jostled his broken finger. He would have to remember to be careful in the future.

Healer Faerra was there to check his injury one last time. When she deemed it sound, Jaax joined his companions as they readied themselves to take flight.

"Wait!" someone cried out, "Don't leave yet!"

The crowd parted and a man, an elf, stumbled forward. His clothes looked stained from the day before and a few scratches marred his face and his pale blond hair was tangled, but other than that, he seemed unhurt.

Jaax turned fully to face him. As he did so he saw the elfin woman trailing after him, and behind her was . . .

The sight of the young girl, the one who had nearly died from the fire that had engulfed half her body, caused Jaax to nearly collapse. She clung to her mother, her eyes downturned, the burns covered in gauze.

"Please, sir dragon, Healer Faerra has done what she can for our daughter, but her wounds are serious and if they become infected . . ."

His voice cracked and tears sprang to his eyes. Jaax grew rigid again, his mouth cut in a grim line. He looked to the healer, but the sad seriousness to her own face acknowledged that she had already done what she could.

"A Morli dragon's fire is different from natural fire," she said softly.

Fire and Ice

Jaax was troubled by her helplessness. This was the same woman who had prodded at a full grown dragon's injury, only to laugh in his face when it had clearly irritated him.

"How do you know this?" he whispered harshly.

Even he, a dragon who had a great knowledge of the Tyrant king and his evil, didn't know that Morli fire was any different than his own. Even Hroombramantu, his mentor and the wisest being he knew, had never mentioned it.

"I know because my method of healing, the same method I use on all my burn victims, always works. There is something about this girl's injuries that I cannot fix."

As terrifying as the information was, Jaax was greatly relieved to learn it. One day he and many others would be called upon to fight these dragons; it was good to know now, before it was too late, that their enemy had an advantage. Still, it was not a comforting thought.

"Lord dragon?"

Jaax shook his head and turned his attention onto the elf's wife. She had moved closer and her daughter had burrowed deeper into her mother's cloak.

"I have heard that you come from a city of magic, a place where extraordinary healers live. Please," she took a shuddering breath, "please take us with you."

"But, your home," Shiroxx spoke up from somewhere behind Jaax.

The woman shook her head sadly. "Destroyed," she said, "along with the shop we owned."

Her husband looked up at Jaax again. "We were jewelers here, very skilled I might say, if my modesty will forgive me. Perhaps we can make a new start in your city?"

Jaax considered this. It would be a small burden to carry three elves back to Lidien, but not impossible. They had nothing left here, except for maybe their friends, but from the way the townspeople held their tongues and eyed the couple and their daughter, Jaax could guess they wouldn't be missed.

And he had failed them terribly. He had allowed the Morli dragon to destroy their home and nearly kill their daughter. He couldn't make amends with all the people of Ahseína, but he could perhaps make amends with the jeweler and his wife. And their daughter.

"Very well, you may travel with us," he said, "but you'll have to learn to hold on tight, and I hope you don't mind a little cold air."

Both the man and the woman smiled brightly, their relief obvious.

"Thank you lord," the jeweler breathed, bowing deeply.

Jaax lifted his injured leg in a gesture of dismissal. "Please, call me Jaax. And what shall I call you?"

"I am Rennor and this is my wife Gracelle and my daughter, Prenne."

The other three dragons had moved closer, all of them sharing their own introductions. It took the elves less than half an hour to gather what was theirs. Most of their belongings had perished in the fire but some items, such as a sturdy cauldron, had survived.

"We use this to make special pieces," Rennor said, patting the cauldron affectionately.

Shiroxx eyed it warily, but eventually snorted softly, dismissing it as of little hindrance. It wasn't too heavy for any of them to carry.

Fire and Ice

Sapheramin and Shiroxx agreed to carry the jeweler and his wife and daughter, while the male dragons offered to carry the large bags that held their equipment. Once everything, and everyone, was settled, the four dragons bid farewell to the people of Ahseína once more and lifted into the sky.

The return journey took longer, what with the need for frequent landings to accommodate the elves. Jaax was eager to get back to Lidien, but his frustration waned whenever the young elfin girl, Prenne, crossed his line of sight. When he remembered her injuries, he made an extra effort to tread lightly. Shiroxx, on the other hand, had no trouble letting her ire show.

"It is taking us twice as long to get back to Lidien!" she hissed at Jaax as he peeled the large travel bags from his back. They had landed in a wide open mountain meadow so that Prenne could get some rest.

Jaax shot his Tanaan companion a poisonous glare. "The girl is terribly injured Shiroxx, we cannot over stress her."

In fact, Jaax thought she might be getting worse, as if the fire of the Morli contained some magical acid that was eating away at her. He shivered.

"All the more reason to hurry!" the female dragon persisted. "The sooner we get back to Lidien, the sooner she can be taken to a powerful healer."

Jaax growled and walked away. There was no arguing with Shiroxx, for the only answer to a problem she ever considered was the solution she had to offer.

They reached Lidien five days later, descending into the sprawling bayside city as the sun was setting over the ocean. Jaax immediately took the elf family to the Academy of Medicine, a series of buildings located at the far northwestern end of the city where the most talented healers from all around Ethöes gathered to practice and study their art.

He felt comfortable leaving the girl in their capable hands and was assured she would make a fine recovery. He left before her family could even thank him. He didn't hold it against them; they had been through much suffering in the last several days and he knew their focus was primarily on their daughter. He only hoped that they were able to establish their business once she was healed.

By the time Jaax returned to his own Lidien home, perched snuggly on a wooded hill overlooking the city, it was nearly midnight. He tried not to wake Neira when he entered, but she heard him nonetheless, climbing downstairs with a candle and dressed in her night robes.

"Master Jaax!" she exclaimed, "You're back! I'll go fix you some tea and something to eat."

"No, please Neira, don't trouble yourself. I am weary and I think I'll just go straight to bed." He smiled. "You can wake me in the morning with one of your famous breakfasts."

Jaax didn't wait for a response, but merely turned down the hallway that led to his study and beyond that, his own personal room. His finger throbbed and his mind was alive with what he had learned in Ahseína.

If the Morli dragons prove to be stronger than we realized, he thought, *then we may not stand a chance . . .*

A shudder coursed through him and as he drifted into a restless sleep. His dreams were haunted with the image of the elfin girl, fire engulfing her as her screams tore through the night. Only it was no longer Prenne who suffered under the Morli's dark, magical fire, but Jahrra, the very one he feared for the most.

Part Two

Jaax sat in his usual position in the front of Essyel Auditorium and listened to a concerned Coalition member drone on and on about how he had never received the proper recognition for some miniscule deed he'd performed.

This cause is not about you! the dragon so desperately wanted to hiss. He clenched his teeth, making his jaw ache, and flexed his fingers. It had been over a month since he'd returned from Ahseína and his broken finger was still a little stiff, but finally healed. It was the scale that healer Faerra had told him would eventually come off that bothered him the most. It pinched his skin between the others, and burned like a raw cut. *It feels like your endless, pointless complaints,* he mused, eyeing the man seeking fame and acknowledgment.

Jaax had been restless ever since his return from Ahseína. His dreams of the burning girl transforming into Jahrra had lessened, but they hadn't gone away completely. It wasn't until a week ago that he realized a trip to Oescienne might be a good idea. *Besides,* he told himself, *it's been at least three years since you last paid your old mentor and his ward a visit; it's about time you returned.* And then he could tell Hroombra, in person, about what had happened in the south of Yddian, about the malicious power of Morli fire.

In actuality, the more Jaax thought about flying south for a day or two, the more he liked the idea. *Soon you'll be needed to join the others on the far side of the Elornn Mountains,* Jaax mused, thinking of his never ending duty of keeping Oescienne's borders safe. *It would be nice to see Jahrra and Hroombra once more before I'm needed elsewhere.*

A sudden, small ache in the Tanaan's injured finger brought his attention back to the babbling Coalition member. Out of habit, he rubbed his other hand over the complaining digit, only to catch the loose scale. He grimaced, and then blanched at the intense worsening of pain. It had been bad timing, for the Resai man had just finished with his plea and now lifted a curious and insulted eyebrow at the Coalition's leader.

Jaax sighed. "You make a valid point-" he paused and gave the man a closer look.

"Chromarre," the man offered with a haughty sniff.

"Chromarre," Jaax finished, almost as an aside. "I will have some of our higher members look into it."

He wouldn't, of course. The man was being ridiculous. But it was best to play things out in a diplomatic manner. Chromarre bowed and sat back down, and then another took his place.

Jaax drew in a deep breath and prepared himself for what remained of an already long, dull day. *I just need to last a few more hours,* he thought, *and then I'll be free to leave for Oescienne.*

He had never been too eager to visit those he had left behind in the southern province, but for some strange reason he could not decipher, the thought of seeing Hroombra, and Jahrra, once again put him in a more agreeable mood all throughout the rest of that day.

* * *

From the sky, the Castle Guard Ruin looked like a great pile of old stones, but Jaax grinned when he caught sight of it, banking his wings so that he could make an easy landing in the great field just to the east. Once on firm ground, the dragon shook and then tucked in his great wings, breathing in a great lungful of the Oescienne air. It made him feel safe, at home. He grinned as old memories pranced through his head, memories of when he was young and when Hroombra had brought him here to live. The

Fire and Ice

Tanaan dragon's smile soon faded, however, when the joyful memories were overrun with the painful ones.

He shook his head. *No,* he thought angrily, *not today, not now.* But it did no good, for the image of the destruction of Ahseína and the young girl burned by the Morli joined those other dark memories, as well as the image of Jahrra taking the place of Prenne in his nightmares.

Jaax gritted his teeth and growled, his lighthearted mood at being in Oescienne again soon replaced with bitterness and anger.

He approached the Castle Guard Ruin with some caution, not wishing to surprise its residents. He poked his head in through the small entrance first, only to smile broadly at the sight he saw. The evil memories could haunt him later; right now he was going to enjoy the company of his old mentor.

"Hroombramantu," he said as cheerily as he could, "do you ever do anything other than sit at that old desk all day and study?"

The ancient Korli dragon, who had had his eyes lowered in concentration, started and glanced up, a look of shock dominating his face. Then he too grinned broadly, his eyes shining. "Jaax! What on Ethöes has brought you to Oescienne? I had no letter from you!"

Jaax's smile softened and he flexed his fingers, which were planted firmly on the ground. His newly healed injury twinged slightly, and he took a deep breath.

"There is something you need to know about, something I fear might prove troublesome in the future."

Hroombra's face fell and his smile vanished.

Jaax swiveled his head. "Is Jahrra around?"

He wondered why she hadn't shown herself yet and he was eager to see her; to see how she had grown since the last time he'd visited three years ago. To see, unlike the image in his nightmares of late, that she was safe and sound.

"She is out with her friends and I am certain they'll be gone most of the day." Hroombra grinned. "Wait until you see how she's grown! But for now, let's get this baleful news out of the way. I'll meet you in the great room."

Jaax nodded once, pulled his head free of the door and walked around to the side of the building where he could enter through a large gap in the wall.

Once the two dragons were settled, Jaax began his tale of what had happened in Ahseína: about the renegade Morli dragon, their battle, and the monster's eventually demise. But it was his description of the effect the fire had on the elfin girl's skin that troubled Hroombra the most. *As it troubles me*, Jaax mused.

Hroombra rubbed his chin in contemplation. "Definitely a problem," he said softly, "but perhaps not so horrifying as we think. Did you speak with the healers after they helped the girl?"

Jaax nodded. "They told me it was partly due to the magic of Ciarrohn, but mostly due to a type of acid that the Morli dragons produce naturally. But," Jaax paused and gave Hroombra a confident look, "they believed it only affects unarmored skin. So if a Nesnan, Resai, elf or human were to protect their skin from exposure, the healers believe they should be relatively safe."

Hroombra sighed. "Well, that is what we'll have to count on for now, until we can learn more."

Before either dragon could say anything else, the hurried sound of hoof beats quickly approaching broke the relative quiet outside.

Jaax gave his old guardian a look and the Korli dragon smiled more brightly than ever.

Fire and Ice

"That would be Jahrra returning with Phrym," he said. "You should see that young colt now, much bigger than when you left him off as a sickly orphan."

Without giving Hroombra a second glance, Jaax rose and quietly exited the ruin from the dragons' entrance. What he saw outside took him by surprise. Sitting atop a fine marble grey stallion was a tall girl with blond hair and a confident set to her shoulders. Her back was to him, but it was clear this child was far different than the one he'd left those few years ago.

Could this really be Jahrra? Where is the timid little girl I last saw?

Just then, two other riders came flying up the trail. Jaax thought they looked familiar, and then he remembered the two Resai siblings who had been with Jahrra the last time he had paid a visit. They were laughing and out of breath.

Jahrra said to her friends, "You two almost beat us!"

The girl then said something about Jahrra and her semequin being too far ahead. Jahrra responded with a laugh, insisting that she and her semequin could have easily been caught.

For some reason or another, Jaax decided that this was his cue to make himself known. He hadn't noticed his scales conforming to the colors of the stones behind him and when he finally did, he felt as if he were spying on the trio of friends.

Clearing his throat, he said in a teasing manner, "No they wouldn't have, you were much too far ahead."

Everyone froze, and then slowly turned to look at him. Jaax's smile, which had been warm and friendly at first, faltered. The two Resai children must have made some movement, because he could hear their horses shifting beneath them. But his attention was fully on Jahrra, the human girl he had found in Crie eleven years ago and had left with Hroombra so that she might remain safe. She glared at him, her blue-grey eyes like ice, and frowned.

Jaax nearly stepped back in shock. He couldn't believe the outright hatred that poured off of her, and suddenly, all of his eagerness at seeing the girl he was responsible for disappeared like a tendril of smoke on a windy day. Burning anger replaced the worry he felt for her and bitterness churned in his stomach instead of joy.

"What are you doing here?" she asked with spite.

His lip curled in irritation. "I'm here on business." *And that is all you need to know for now, until your attitude changes.*

"Where's master Hroombra?" she pressed.

"He'll be out soon," Jaax replied coolly, then feeling particularly spiteful, he added, "After hearing your approach, I thought I'd come see what all the shouting was about. Tell me Jahrra, do you always enjoy deceiving your friends?"

It was harsh, Jaax knew that, but he had a bad habit of turning nasty when anyone was rude to him. Jahrra blanched as she tightened the hold on her reins. *So*, he thought with a satisfied smirk, *that hit a nerve, did it?*

Jaax let Jahrra seethe in the cesspit she had created around herself and instead turned to the two Resai siblings, Gieaun and Scede, Jaax suddenly recalled. He offered them a warm greeting and when Scede asked about his ability to create fire, the Tanaan dragon eagerly put on a show, complete with smoke rings.

Just as he suspected, Jahrra climbed down from Phrym and in a fit of anger marched off towards the old stables several yards away. He asked the Resai siblings if she was always so ill-mannered, but when they looked at him as if he had suddenly grown another set of wings, he shook his head and mumbled something about forgetting the whole thing.

Jaax felt a small pang of guilt for the way he had spoken to Jahrra. He had been ready to ask all about her adventures and

Fire and Ice

what she had learned in school and everything else he had missed out on her entire life. But that look of disgust and hatred in her eyes had forced him to throw up a wall, one that he had used frequently throughout his life when anyone ever tried to get close to him. Or whenever anyone tried to get close enough to injure him.

I just never thought I'd have to use it against you, he thought bitterly as he watched Jahrra traipse up the sloping field, kicking at clumps of grass along the way. He furrowed his brow, wondering what on Ethöes could have caused such anger against him. *Whatever it is, I don't know if I'll have the time during this visit to get to the root of it. Until then, I'll just offer her the same courtesy she offers me.* Jaax's lip curled in delightful challenge. *Oh yes, this should be an interesting visit after all . . .*

* * *

The loud chatter of arguing birds drew Jaax from his sleep the following morning. He groaned and reached up to rub his head, wondering why it ached so badly. Sighing, he blinked his eyes and looked around at the unfamiliar settings. He wasn't in his own room in Lidien, but in a much smaller space with a large fireplace and a sizeable gap in one wall . . . Ah, the Castle Guard Ruin. That was when the memories of the day before came flooding back: his discussion about the Morli dragon with Hroombra, Jahrra's cold greeting, and then what had happened after that . . .

Jaax grimaced as he recalled the memory. As Jahrra had been returning Phrym to his stable, Scede had let it slip that the three of them had been hunting unicorns earlier in the day. Jaax had snorted at first. How absurd. Unicorns hadn't been seen in Oescienne since the fall of the humans five hundred years ago. But Hroombra had brightened at the boy's claim.

When Jahrra eventually returned she had been very reluctant to give up any information. This, for some reason or another, rubbed Jaax the wrong way and when she was pressed, he suspected she hadn't told them the whole truth. He just knew there was more to the story than what she had told them.

Which explains my foul mood this morning, he thought bitterly. The sun was still a long way off from rising, so Jaax decided on an early morning flight over the Wreing Florenn to help ease his nerves and maybe scout for evidence of Jahrra's ridiculous claim. He didn't believe her. Not only because what she had said was so unbelievable, but because he was certain she was being dishonest.

He gritted his teeth as he spread his wings and climbed into the dark sky. It was that dishonesty that ate at him the most. Had Hroombra raised her to be deceitful? In Jaax's mind, that would be the worst possible thing he could have done for the girl.

During his hour-long flight, he spotted nothing stirring in the Wreing Florenn that he thought could be considered suspicious. But during his time away from the Ruin, he had come up with a solution to his problem with Jahrra. He and Hroombra had discussed it, late into the night, and had considered enrolling her in defense lessons with a pair of reclusive elves. Now Jaax was convinced that this would help give Jahrra some discipline in her life. *And it wouldn't hurt if she knew how to fight and defend herself,* he thought as he touched down silently in the field beside the Ruin.

Before he took her there, however, he wanted to see what she knew on her own. *And this way,* he mused, *I can thoroughly prove to her that she will need these lessons.* Jahrra would hate him for it, but it was for her own good. *Besides, she already hates me. Can't get any worse.*

As he anticipated, Jahrra was not happy about being dragged out of bed so early in the morning, but Jaax was

Fire and Ice

determined so he didn't once soften his treatment of her. He took her to an abandoned field further down the road and then instructed her to try and get past his guard. Jahrra was appalled at this, but she did as she was told, charging at the looming dragon with nothing but a large branch to defend herself. Twice Jaax was able to overpower her, growling instructions on how to better make contact with her make-shift sword.

He dropped her after having grabbed the stick, but as she landed she was immediately charging him again. Jaax, caught off guard, moved to lift back up on his hind legs, but he wasn't fast enough. Jahrra struck him with her branch, hard, directly on the knuckle of his newly healed broken finger.

He sucked in a sharp breath as a lancing pain shot through his finger. He cursed himself inwardly, believing that she had managed to break his finger again. *Serves you right,* he thought to himself, *this is what you get for being so hard on her.*

Jaax shook his hand out, and then reluctantly examined it, blinking in surprise. The scale that had been loose for weeks, causing him more annoyance than anyone deserved, was gone.

Barely, Jaax could hear Jahrra's concerned voice.

"Oh Jaax! I'm sorry!"

He looked up and saw genuine guilt there. Her eyes, which for the past day had held only cold rejection and loathing, now shone with sympathy.

Against his will, he gave her a small smile. "Don't worry, that scale has been threatening to come off for weeks."

Suddenly, all the tension and hard feelings that had existed between them seemed to fade a little, and as Jahrra searched out the wayward scale, Jaax felt his own worries ease.

Jahrra found the scale and returned it to Jaax, and he managed to hold onto it even as they made their journey towards the foothills behind town where Jahrra would meet her new trainers, the elves of Dhonoara.

* * *

The flight home to Lidien took Jaax a little over two days, but that gave him plenty of time to think about all he had learned on his short visit. He had left Jahrra in the capable hands of his elvin friends and had flown directly from their secluded cabin in order to make his way back to the City of Light.

Jaax grinned at the memory. Jahrra hadn't liked his abrupt departure, and if he didn't know any better, he would have said she was disappointed in the fact that he couldn't stay and visit longer.

No, I won't flatter myself, he mused, *you were just angry that I left you with strangers.*

Jaax now sat cozily in his great room, sipping Neira's delicious tea and getting ready for another day in Emehriel Hall before leaving once again to scout the borders of Oescienne for the Tyrant's minions and spies. *At least Jahrra is safe for now,* he thought.

He let his mind wander back to the short visit he had paid his distant ward and her guardian, Jahrra's sharp eyes and strong spirit reminding him very much of fire and ice. *Both of which can burn you in their own cruel way if you don't treat them with the respect they deserve.* Jaax let out a breath, one he hadn't realized he had been holding. He knew that in the future he would have to find a way to show Jahrra the respect she deserved, without forfeiting the esteem he deserved as well. Someday in the distant future, he hoped the two of them would learn to work together, for it was clear the Crimson King had quite a menagerie of soldiers awaiting those who would dare challenge him. *And we will challenge him Jahrra,* Jaax thought morosely as he glanced out the window onto the rainy day, *we must.*

Fire and Ice

Shaking the wayward thoughts from his mind and gritting his teeth, Jaax turned his head to study the small wooden box that lay on the carpet between his feet. Inside was the scale Jahrra had managed to remove from his injured finger, the same scale that had bothered him since the incident in Ahseína over a month ago. Somehow, he had managed to hold onto it between Oescienne and Felldreim. It wasn't one of his larger, more colorful scales, but it was just the right size to serve as a pendant for a necklace. *And what a better way to reward her for besting a dragon?*

The stormy day would be filled with the boring complaints of diplomats and simple shop owners as they came before the Coalition to either offer help or make their grievances known. But before he went to work, Jaax had an errand to run, hopefully one that would bring him more enjoyment than what the rest of the day offered.

Jaax grinned. *Yes, a pendant on a silver chain would be very nice. And I know just the people who can do the job for me . . .*

* * *

Jaax stared down the narrow alley way and frowned in disappointment. The people at the Academy of Medicine had gladly given him the address to the jeweler's new shop, but they hadn't informed him that a dragon could not fit between the tall buildings.

A merchant's servant came strolling down the lane, whistling a happy tune, oblivious to his surroundings until he spotted the looming dragon standing in front of him.

"I wonder if I could ask you a favor," he said to the young boy, hoping his smile translated as a friendly one.

The young Nesnan boy gaped, then swallowed, but nodded his head in agreement.

"I need to speak with the owner of the jewelry shop, and as you can see, I cannot go myself without knocking down these fine buildings."

Jaax read the address to the jeweler's out loud, and then watched as the boy disappeared down the alley. Less than five minutes later, the blond elf came bursting out of one of the doors towards the end of the row of buildings. His face was alit with a warm smile as he approached the dragon.

"Master Raejaaxorix! You have found our shop, I see."

Jaax returned the greeting, and then became distracted when the jeweler's wife and daughter joined his side. To the dragon's great relief, Prenne looked whole once again. Terrible scars marred one side of her body, but she was smiling up at him and didn't seem to be in pain.

"What brings you to our side of the city in this weather?" Rennor asked, gesturing towards the dark clouds.

The dragon smiled again. "I wish to commission you for a job."

Jaax produced the box and described the necklace he wished for them to make.

The jeweler nodded, grinning from ear to ear. "It shall be an honor and a special challenge for us. We've never been asked to make a pendant out of a dragon's scale! But I don't see how it could be much different than creating a clasp for a crystal."

He held the scale up to the dim light and pursed his mouth in thought, nodded once, then put the scale safely back in the box.

"It shall be complete by this afternoon. I'll have a mail carrier drop it off at your residence by the end of the day."

Jaax raised his scaly brow, surprised that it would be ready so soon, then simply nodded his head and gave the jeweler the directions to his home.

Fire and Ice

"Do you have any ideas about how it should be set?" Rennor asked before he turned to return to his shop.

Jaax shook his head. "No, I think any design you come up with will suffice."

Then he thought of Jahrra and how she seemed to be averse to anything overly feminine. He grinned. "Though she might appreciate something more on the simple side."

"She?" the jeweler inquired.

"Yes," Jaax answered, "it's for a young girl, a few years younger than your daughter, perhaps. She is, she's . . ."

Jaax fished for an answer, but was unable to come up with a good way to describe his relationship with Jahrra. A friend? Not quite. His ward? Sort-of. The human child he had been charged to find and protect? Yes, but he couldn't say that.

"Someone special," Gracelle answered with a warm smile, hugging her daughter close.

Jaax grinned. "Yes, someone special indeed."

The Tanaan dragon nodded his head to each elf in turn, and then headed back into the heart of the city, where the various members of the Coalition of Ethöes waited his attendance.

The meeting was a lengthy and dull one and by the time Jaax had returned home, it was long past sunset. Neira met him at the great door, grinning widely.

"A courier dropped off something for you. I put it on the desk in your study. I hope you don't mind," she said.

"Of course not," Jaax answered tiredly.

He wished Neira a good night, and then headed into his own chambers at the opposite end of the large mansion. He carefully lit the candles and a fire in the hearth, then sat down and eyed the brown paper package dubiously. Very carefully, he unwrapped the delicate parcel to find an intricately carved box, not the one he had originally placed the scale in, and sighed. It was a beautiful piece and when he opened the lid, his wonder and admiration only grew.

Carefully, he lifted the delicate-looking chain and let it slip over two fingers, the pendent nestling carefully in the palm of his hand. The chain was a unique silvery gold metal that sparkled in the firelight, and the very top of the scale had been set in a clasp composed of the same metal. It was a very simple design, but very beautiful as well.

Jaax had thought of sending the pendent to Jahrra as soon as it was finished, but now he felt that he would save it for the next time he visited, to give it to her himself.

He moved to return the pendent safely to its box, but paused when he noticed the note tucked beneath it. All it said was: *For your kindness and bravery in Ahseína, and for keeping our daughter with us.*

Jaax frowned. He already had a small pouch full of coins ready to give to the jeweler and his family for their fine work, but they had not named a price.

Very well, he thought with a grin, *I shall have Neira find someone to deliver it in the morning. By the time it reaches your shop, I'll be long gone, gliding over the mountains of the east in search of more enemies to thwart.*

As Jaax returned the necklace to its box, he felt his mouth quirk in a smile again, for a white-gold streak shimmered down the silver chain as it reflected the fire in the hearth. *Fire and ice,* he mused, *just like the spirit of our young girl, Jahrra.* And she would need that burning spirit of hers when fate finally called her, Jaax was certain of it.

PRONUNCIATION GUIDE

Ahseína - AH-say-nuh

Dathian - DA-thee-en

Denaeh - di-NAY-uh

Ellysian - uh-LISS-ee-an

Ethöes - ETH-oh-es

Eydeth - AY-deth

Faerra - FARE-uh

Gieaun - JOON

Gracelle - Gra-SELL

Hroombramantu -HROOM-bruh-mon-too

Jahrra - JAIR-uh

Kihna - KEE-nuh

Lidien - LI-dee-en

Pahrdh - PARD

Prenne - PREN

Raejaaxorix - RAY-jax-or-ix

Rennor - REN-or

Rhudedth - ROO-dedth

Sapheramin - SA-fare-uh-min

Scede - SADE

Shiroxx - SHEE-rox

Tollorias - toe-LORE-ee-us

Yddian - ID-ee-an

ABOUT THE AUTHOR

Jenna Elizabeth Johnson grew up and still resides on the Central Coast of California, the very place where the Legend of Oescienne first began to blossom into the epic it has become. "The province of Oescienne is based primarily on the topography of this area, and some specific locations in the novel reflect actual sites. These places are dear to me, and I wanted to share their natural magic with those who might read my books."

Miss Johnson has a BA in Art Practice with a minor in Celtic Studies from the University of California at Berkeley. It was during her time in college that she decided to begin her first novel, "I had these stories stored away in my head and had even sketched out some ideas during my studio time. One day it dawned upon me that if I didn't write these stories down, then I would be the only one ever to enjoy them. Furthermore, reading such works as Beowulf, The Mabinogi and The Second Battle of Maige Tuired in my Scandinavian and Celtic Studies courses only added fuel to the fire."

Having a degree in art has also aided her in the creation of the world of Ethöes. The cover images, the map of Oescienne and all of the artwork found on her website, www.oescienne.com, was done by the author. "Having a picture, especially a map, helps me to visualize the story more completely. I hope that the images I have placed on my site will help my readers get a better idea of what my world looks like. Of course, you are always welcome to disregard them if the images you have in your head are better than the ones I offer."

Besides writing and drawing, Miss Johnson enjoys reading, gardening, camping, archery and hiking. She also loves animals and bird watching and has many bird feeders set up in her garden at home.

Jenna Elizabeth Johnson is currently working on several other book projects, including future novels in the Oescienne series. You can contact her through her website: www.jennaelizabethjohnson.com

Other books in the *Legend of Oescienne*
series:

The Finding (Book One)
The Beginning (Book Two)
The Awakening (Book Three)

* * * * *

And be sure to check out the author's
new YA, Paranormal Romance series,
the *Otherworld Trilogy*:
Faelorehn (Book One)
Dolmarehn (Book Two)
Luathara (Book Three)

For more information, including maps, news, illustrations
and how to contact the author, visit:
www.oescienne.com
or
www.jennaelizabethjohnson.com

A Sneak Peek at the first book in the *Legend of Oescienne* series:

THE FINDING

-Prologue-
Evasion

Morning's first light poured into a cramped, dank cave casting strange shadows against its distorted walls. It was a very ordinary cave as caves go, and up until a few days ago it seemed things would remain that way. The cave had sat empty in a cliff above the western sea, left alone to inhale the ocean's salty air and capture the sound of the waves crashing below. Hidden and unseen in a cove only a few knew about, the cave had remained empty for so many years. But that was all about to change.

A piercing beam of light fought its way through a narrow hole in the ceiling of the cavern breaking into the empty chamber and making the sunlight flooding through its mouth seem dimmer. The ray came to rest upon the pale face of a figure bunched upon the cold, dirty floor like a pile of discarded rags. His eyes were closed in sleep, but the silent expression on his face was far from restful. His dark hair was unkempt and his face appeared almost bloodless. He was as still as death, but his tense features and the grim cut of his mouth confirmed the struggle that only the living possessed.

The man stirred awake and rolled onto his side, sending a scraping and soft groaning sound playing against the curved walls. Wincing and gasping in pain, he clutched his shoulder and dragged himself up into a sitting position. The bright beam of light was now slanted across his profile, illuminating the distinct characteristics of his race. His fine features and narrow, sharply tapered ears proved that he was of elfin descent, but it was his dark hair, pale skin and uncommonly tall stature that revealed him as one of the Aellheian elves of the east.

He blinked his eyes as the waves of pain ebbed and passed, looking blankly around the natural room that he'd been sleeping in. The cave was littered with jagged stalactites and stalagmites, making it resemble the mouth of a yawning dragon. Several conical tunnels were scattered throughout, giving the impression that a giant had pressed its fingers into the small space while it was still a soft cavity of clay, leaving their indentations behind.

The injured elf breathed deeply as he recalled climbing up here only a few days before. He was grateful despite the exhausting effort; at least now he could rest easy. This place was a great secret not known to his pursuers. He closed his eyes and tried to clear his mind. A sharp, metallic taste in his mouth forced him to recall the skirmish he'd had not long ago, the one that had landed him in his current situation. He sighed and rested his head against the wall, listening to the low rumble of the waves outside as he tried to distract himself from the endless sound of dripping water echoing throughout the cave. The smell of saltwater and pine resin, dust and distant fog hung in the air like a delicate feather, reminding him of the thick forest perched on the edge of the cliffs just above his head.

Despite his hot skin and the relatively relaxing rhythm of the crashing waves, the elf felt a cold chill clenching his heart. He ran his fingers through his tangled hair as if this action might comb away the grogginess and pounding headache that seemed to swallow him. He'd been in this place for three days now, or so he thought, and he feared the wound in his shoulder might be infected. He'd cleaned it and treated it with an herbal balm, but it was swollen and throbbing.

For several months he'd managed to evade the Tyrant's men but now it seemed they'd finally caught their prey. He'd gone so far as to enter the land west of the feared Thorbet and Elornn mountains, a place the Crimson King would never go, but it was clear the Tyrant's soldiers thought differently. They'd finally moved in close enough to place an arrow deep in his shoulder just to the left of his heart. Desperate, injured and out of options, he headed further west towards a land he'd once considered home only to find a familiar place of sanctuary. This particular cave would hide him well, but he also knew that if he died here so would the secrets he carried.

The elf trembled again, blinking against the harsh light hitting his face. Whether the shivering was a result of an encroaching fever or from the thought of his world crashing down around him, he couldn't tell. He drew a long, deep breath and carefully pulled a leather-bound journal, a pen and an inkwell out of the saddle bags he'd had the sense to grab before fleeing on foot. He propped himself up against the wall, quietly thanking Ethöes it was smooth, and leaned forward so that one of the empty pages of the journal lit up to a blinding white from the sunbeam pouring through the roof. He thought for a while as he continued to fight off the sickening heat emanating from his shoulder. After several moments of reverie, he dipped his quill into the inkwell and began to write:

It has been three centuries and more since the world changed, but not much has happened since. Whether that fact bodes good or ill towards the people loyal to the Goddess, I cannot tell. The pages before this tell the story of the world and how Ethöes created all the living and nonliving things that exist upon its surface, of the rise of the god Ciarrohn and Traagien's defeat of him, of the folly of the elves and the creation of the humans and their eventual end.

All of the pages before this one hold that story and the secrets of the royal family of Oescienne.

Therefore I, the last Magehn of the Tanaan king, will not waste time with the tales of old. What I can tell you, however, is that three hundred years ago the Crimson King cast a terrible curse upon the last race of humans, transforming them into dragons and severing their link to the province of Oescienne. From that point on, the tie between the western province and its rightful sovereigns, the race of humans, was destroyed, setting in motion the Tyrant's first steps in clearing the way for the complete domination of all seven provinces of Ethöes.

A muffled shout followed by a torrent of angry words brought the Magehn's pen to a stop. His heart quickened its pace and the throbbing in his head and shoulder fell into rhythm with it. The noise came from above, and through the tiny skylight in his cave the elfin man could barely make out the foreign tongue of several of the Tyrant's men. He hoped they wouldn't find his horse, but then he remembered he'd removed its bridle and saddle, encouraging the animal to flee just before he made his way down the narrow trail leading to his hiding place.

Although he couldn't decipher what it was the men said, the Magehn knew that they'd tracked him this far. *How they found the courage to cross the mountains is beyond me,* he thought bitterly. Then he realized it hadn't been courage but fear. Those loyal to the Crimson King may have feared the far western mountains, but they feared their king more.

The elf listened silently as the voices trailed off. When he was certain they had moved on to search for him in some other location, he got back to his work, focusing on finishing while he still could:

Though the humans are now dragons, and those dragons are now scattered, there is reason yet to hope. The Tyrant still suffers from the wounds inflicted upon him in that final battle with the last Tanaan prince and his people; he still struggles to regain his strength from the effort it took to transform them. Yet no one knows when the Crimson King will regain his former might and attack the remaining provinces. Most believe it is only a matter of time, and time is running short.

The last Tanaan prince is now lost. Many claim he is long dead, for wouldn't he have returned to his people and rallied them by now, even in their reptilian forms? Yet I saw his transformation and witnessed his escape within the confusion of the aftermath of the great battle. I believe with all of my heart, though I may not live out my immortal existence as I had once hoped, that a day will come when the Tyrant's curse is lifted and the Tanaan humans will return to rule in Oescienne once again.

The elf halted his hand, staring down at the stark black marks he'd sketched upon the paper. He was writing in his native language, the language of the Dhonoaran elves, descendents of the Aellheians. He should have felt pride for their development of such a beautiful language, but instead he felt a bitter taste of disgust rise in his throat. So much sorrow, so much pain, destruction and avaricious betrayal had come from his people that it brought him some shame, even though he knew it wasn't his fault.

The Magehn drew a sharp breath as a sudden stab of pain ripped down his arm. He had been about to continue his notation but instead he paused, his jaw clenched, willing the ache to pass. As he waited in agony, he returned his thoughts to the ugly circumstances of his world. Instead of thinking of his ancient elfin ancestors, however, he recalled his own loved ones harmed or corrupted by the Tyrant King. He thought especially of the one whose trust he'd lost, someone who was still dear to him. Soon he felt another pain, a pain that would never heal. The ache in his shoulder and the ache in his heart mingled, combining to form one great pang of anguish.

The elf took a deep breath, suppressing the distracting memories that were now surfacing in his mind. *I don't have time to tell my own story. I have time only for this* . . . He forced his screaming thoughts to the back of his mind and continued on with what he had started. Beads of sweat broke out on his forehead, but he wrote on:

I have spent long years mourning my king and my people, but I could not hide from the terrors of this world forever. I came out of my hiding no more than six months ago, and it took the blessed words of hope to make me finally face my fears. I knew the Tyrant searched for me, that he seeks vengeance, even now. He is aware that I hold the secrets of the Tanaan and believes that I know the location of their prince. But I braved his wrath and went forth into the world despite the great danger, for I had received word of something amazing, something extraordinary.

Before I was tracked down and wounded by the Tyrant's minions, I had been riding throughout all of Ethöes, spreading this great news, news of an answer to our plight. The Oracles, those that still remain with us, spoke of a miracle promised by Ethöes herself, one that could mean the salvation of our world.

Pain beyond description flared through the elf's fevered body. He cried out in anguish as his pen dragged across the bottom of the white paper leaving a long, jagged black line. This ache was worse than the ones before, and it struck fear into the Magehn's heart. His eyes watered and his vision became fuzzy as he wondered about the origin of the arrow that had caused this wound. Perhaps it had been poisoned. He felt lightheaded and sensed his mind being pulled in and out of consciousness. Furiously, and with fresh determination, the last Magehn of the

Tanaan king began writing as fast as he could, able to produce one more sentence before he knew no more:

I have done what I can to spread this new prophecy throughout the land, a prophecy about the return of a lasting peace, a prophecy about a lost prince, and a prophecy about a young, pure-blooded human girl born to save us all.